Murder in Loft 36: A Tempest Danvers Supernatural Tale

Shannon McRoberts

Published by Rogue Goddess Productions, 2023.

MURDER IN LOFT 36: A TEMPEST DANVERS SUPERNATURAL TALE

First edition. July 1, 2023.

Copyright © 2023 Shannon McRoberts.

ISBN: 979-8215065372

Written by Shannon McRoberts.

Table of Contents

Chapter 1: 10 Years Earlier

"TEMPEST! STOP DAYDREAMING and grab me a bag of flour from the dry stores room." My mother's voice sliced through my concentration, snapping me back to reality. I glanced at the clock groaning when I realized the display read 10 as in AM. It was going to be a very long day. I stood up from my favorite spot next to the window, but I was sure to leave my notebook and pens spread on the table to ward off any table snatchers.

Sunday was a slow day at Xpress, my mother's café in downtown Frankfort. Most of the surrounding businesses were closed or didn't open until after lunch on Sunday. I never understood the reasoning behind the weird hours. My mom thought the practice was charming and unique to living in a small town. I saw it as nothing more than a loss of income. If more stores opened early on Sunday, more people would be out and wanting to eat at Xpress, almost like a symbiotic relationship. Unfortunately, I found myself to be too much of a progressive thinker when it came to the ideals of our little town.

Shuffling through the double doors leading into the kitchen, I turned right and headed down the small hallway containing the café's dry goods. Opening the door, the light automatically clicked on, where rows of neatly stacked storage shelves greeted me. My mom could be a bit on the OCD side when left to her own devices. Once, during one of our family therapy sessions, I heard our therapist say the OCD tendencies come from her need to feel in control because that's how she deals with the trauma of losing my dad.

I was only two when someone shot and killed my dad in a robbery gone wrong. I don't really remember him, but everyone tells me he was one of the best cops they have ever met. Of course, I wouldn't know. My mom, though, remembers my dad. In fact, the reason she obsessively makes sure she has everything stocked is because she blames herself for his death. If she had planned better, she wouldn't have run out of the special sugar she needed to finish the tart she had to turn in the next morning for her dessert class. That's why dad was at that store the night robbers shot him, because mom needed the sugar and asked him to stop on his way home. He didn't die in a hero's blaze of glory. He died in aisle nine while bending over to grab the bag of sugar. One robber freaked out when they saw him and shot him in the back.

I grabbed a bag of flour from the shelf in one hand, pulling the row forward with the other. Before updating the inventory sheet, I counted seven small bags of flour remaining. I hated my mother's inventory system, but it helped her sleep at night, so I begrudgingly followed her rules. Opening the door, I went back into the kitchen. My mom stood in front of her mixer, staring at the machine.

"Here's your flour, Mom," I said as I sat the bag down on the counter. "Mom, are you OK?"

She ran her fingers under her eyes and quickly rubbed them onto her green apron before turning. "Nothing is wrong, sugar. The mixer is acting up again, is all. It blew some flour into my eyes earlier. I was trying to wash the particles out with eye drops. I don't know what's wrong with this crazy thing."

"Mom, your mixer is less than a month old. You need to take it back to Sam and have him turn it in on warranty. You can't run a business with an unreliable mixer."

My mom looked up at me and smiled. Her deep green eyes twinkled in the fluorescent lighting. "I know, Tempest, I know. I'll call down to Sam's store when he opens on Monday."

"How are you going to make anything for tomorrow? See, this is why stores should be open on Sunday! You're going to miss the morning rush if you can't pre-make your dough today. Do you realize how much money you will lose?"

Mom shook her head, causing strands of her brown hair to come untucked from her messy bun. "Tempy, it's fine, honey. I'll make extra streusel bites for tomorrow and run a special. People will understand. Sam will probably give me a new mixer and I can make donuts for Tuesday. It will work out."

My mother's overly perky reassurance grated on my nerves. I took deep breaths, like Mrs. Ansel, our therapist, instructed. I didn't need therapy for anything I was going through. Rather, the therapy was more for me to learn how to cope with my mom and her trauma. But, sometimes, the strategies Mrs. Ansel taught Mom came in handy for me. My annoyance suddenly dropped away when I heard the bell on the front door jingle, indicating someone had come into the shop. I took the jingle as a welcome distraction and darted out to the front of the shop. I laughed when I saw who stood in the store.

"Mr. Cardinal, what a surprise. I was telling Mom she needed to call you." I leaned onto the counter, propping myself up on my elbows.

Sam's face turned red as he cleared his throat. "Really, why would you tell her to call me Tempest?"

I smiled as Sam squirmed. I suspected he harbored a major crush on Mom, but he was too shy to ask her out on a date. The redness in his face confirmed what I guessed all along. "Her mixer is on the fritz again. She won't be able to make her dough for tomorrow's morning rush."

Sam frowned. "That mixer is barely a month old. You say this isn't the first time it's had an issue? Why didn't she tell me?"

As if on cue, Elizabeth Danvers exited the kitchen and waltzed into the front store of her café. She had taken off the green apron and pulled down her messy bun. "I didn't tell you, Sam, because I could fix the problem myself. I figured it was something silly I did, but I don't know what's wrong with it now. Tempy was urging me to call you as soon as I could."

"I'm so sorry, Elizabeth. I didn't know you had any issues. I can fetch you a replacement today."

My mom threw up her hands and shook her head. "No, it's OK. I plan on running a special on streusel bites tomorrow, anyway. If you can have the mixer for me by lunchtime tomorrow, that would be perfect."

Sam smiled and nodded his head. "I can have the mixer here first thing after Reginald gets in."

The two smiled stupidly at each other for a moment before I cleared my throat. "Is there something I can get you, Mr. Cardinal?"

Sam's head snapped in my direction as he raised a brow. "Get me?"

"Yeah, you came into the café, so I assumed you wanted something to eat. Maybe one of those egg sandwiches on a bagel?"

"Oh, yeah, I almost forgot why I stopped by." Sam turned as he pulled out two pieces of paper and offered them to Mom.

Mom tilted her head and squinted at the small slips of paper. "What is that, Sam?"

"I got tickets to the Paper Mache Band. They are going to be playing next Saturday night at the amphitheater down by the river. I thought you might want to go with me. My daughter, Maria, she's not into the same music I am these days."

A frown crossed mom's face as she shook her head. "I don't know, Sam. That would require me to stay out late. I've never left Tempy alone at night."

Before making a loud noise, I rolled my eyes. "Mom, I'm fifteen! I can stay home for a few hours. You should go listen to the old people music. All you do is work. It's time for you to have some FUN!"

Mom let out a shaky laugh while she twirled the ends of her hair. "Look, I'd like to go with you, but I'm not comfortable leaving Tempy alone."

Sam's head hung as his shoulders slumped. "I understand. I'll use the tickets as a prize at the shop."

I gritted my teeth. There had to be some way to guarantee my mom would go. All she did was work, and Sam seemed like such a nice guy. I was almost an adult, but my mom had the hardest time letting me out of her sight. Perhaps deploying some psychology into the situation would help. "Wait, Mr. Cardinal, didn't you say you had a daughter? Who stays with her while you go out late at night? Maybe they could stay with me and her?"

"My daughter is a smidge older than you, Tempest. She's seventeen and if I must be out of the house, I can leave her on her own. She can drive, she's trained in CPR, and she's a babysitter herself."

A feeling of joy shot through me as I clapped my hands. "Well, there you go, Mom. Problem solved. Sam's daughter can stay with me and you two can go out!"

At the suggestion, Sam perked up. "That is a good idea. You could take Tempest to my place, and she could stay with Maria, since I live close to the venue. I also have a guest house if you two wanted to stay after the concert. I know you don't live far away, but there's no reason to drive home tired since I have extra space."

"That sounds great, Sam! We could make a weekend out of it. Mom, we could pretend we were vacationing and renting one of those houses in a small town like those people on the show." I hoped my enthusiasm would help my mom ease into this idea. I didn't need someone to stay with me and she didn't need to punish herself over Dad anymore.

"Fine. Since you are so adamant about this, Tempy. I will let you stay at Sam's and go to the concert. OK?"

Jumping up, I pumped my fist in the air. "Woo! Yeah! Mom's going on a date."

Sam blushed while my mom shook her head at my display.

"Honestly, Tempy, must you make such a spectacle of yourself?" Mom asked as she turned towards Sam. "What time should we show up?"

"The concert starts at 7PM, so you and Tempest can come around 5:30 and we can eat dinner together."

"Alright, Sam, I will see you tomorrow when you bring me my new mixer."

Sam nodded his head. "Yes, ma'am. I look forward to seeing you on Friday, Elizabeth."

Chapter 2

After a long week of work at the shop, I looked forward to our little getaway at Sam's. I bolted out of the car and ran into the house to shower before my mom could wheedle out of her date. I broke my record of world's fastest shower by being out and dried off before my mom knocked on the bathroom door.

"Tempy, did you wash behind your ears?"

I wrapped myself in my towel and yanked the door open. "Yes, Mom! I'm fifteen, not six. I know how to shower."

Mom stood in the hallway wringing her hands. "I know, Tempy, but I...I want to make a good impression."

Holding my towel secure with one hand, I reached out with my other hand, placing it on top of my mom's hands. "Mom, the cleanliness of my ears has nothing to do with how much Sam Cardinal likes you. He's been into you for the last four years."

My mom's mouth fell open as she jerked her hand away from mine in her best shocked southern lady act. "Tempest Danvers! The forwardness of your statement is a little much for a proper young lady."

A snort escaped my nose. "Really, Mom?"

She shrugged as a smile exploded on her face. She didn't smile often, but when she did, it was an incredible sight.

"We're going to be late if we don't hurry. I left you plenty of hot water." I moved to walk out of the bathroom as I motioned for Mom to enter. Even though our house was spacious for us, it was older and only had one full bathroom. We bought the house from a man who made his living flipping older houses. The renovations and additions gave the house a modern yet nostalgic atmosphere. Mom didn't care about the single bathroom because the kitchen in this house was to die for. In fact, the kitchen took up most of the first floor. Our bedrooms were on the second floor, on either side of the communal bathroom.

I flung my bedroom door open with a shove of my foot. I didn't worry about closing it behind me because my closet was to the right of the door. It wasn't like anyone could see me in all my glory. The windows in my room were the long, skinny type with blinds. They reminded me of something in a hotel room, but the remodeler told me they were fancy windows called *jalousie*. I personally think the remodeler just used some old windows he had lying around.

Rummaging in my closet, I manage to find a clean pair of jeans and an over-sized t-shirt. I didn't care much about the order of my clothes. Heck, I didn't care much about fashion at all. I found the girls in my school obsessed with designer clothes rather silly. For me, if it was clean, I would wear it.

I grabbed two more shirts and two more pairs of jeans to toss into my duffle bag, not caring if the garments would wrinkle or not. It was clear, by how I packed, I didn't harbor the same OCD tendencies of my mother. She would fold everything in her case with care.

I moved from the closet to my dresser, where I pulled out several pairs of socks and undergarments. Tossing those items into the bag, I turned and looked at my writing desk. Sighing, I contemplated whether I should take my notebook and pens. I didn't want to appear anti-social, but what would I do if I didn't hit it off with Maria? I had never met her, and she was older than me. She could have been one of those trendy girls who caused me to roll my eyes so hard it felt as if they would rip out of my head. Plus, what would I do if inspiration struck for a story? Giving in to the what if, I grabbed my notebook and pen case, shoving them into the duffle before pulling the zipper to shut the bag.

Satisfied I was ready to go, I walked out of my room and into the hallway. My mom stood in the bathroom's doorway wrapped in a towel. She had a pained look on her face.

"Mom, are you almost ready to go?"

Her eyes turned towards me, her face blank.

I snapped my fingers and yelled at her. "Mom, are you OK?"

Blinking many times, my mom came back from whatever far off place she had been only moments ago. "Yes, honey, I was lost in thought for a minute."

I crossed my arms over my chest. "Uh, huh. You mean you were planning out all the horrible scenarios of how things could go wrong?"

Her face flushed as she looked down at the floor. "Why does it sometimes seem as if you are the parent and I'm the child?"

I walked up to her and wrapped my arms around her waist. "Mom, don't worry all the time. You and I will have a fabulous time tonight. Remember what Mrs. Ansel told us last week?"

Patting me on top of the head, I heard Mom counting. "You're right Tempy. I'll be ready in ten minutes. Are you all packed?"

I released my mom's waist and pointed to my bag. "Yup, I'm ready to go. I'll go put my duffle in the car and meet you in the living room, OK?"

Mom nodded, and I released her before grabbing my duffle and charging out the front door. Flinging open the back car door, I shoved my bag onto the bench seat. A warm breeze blew, causing me to stop and take in a deep breath. The one thing I had to say about living in Kentucky was the weather was weird. Although it was a few days before Halloween, it was still warm enough to be outside without a coat. I wouldn't so much as need a light coat for the entire weekend, even though I had one in the car just in case. My mom always packed emergency coats, jackets, blankets, and other supplies in the trunk of our blue sedan. My mom may have been riddled with anxiety since my dad's death, but her planning helped her to always be prepared.

Hearing the front door close, I realized I had forgotten to go back into the house. I looked up to find Mom frowning as she double checked the door.

"Tempy, there you are! I was worried something had happened to you."

I looked down at the ground and kicked at an acorn in the driveway. "Sorry, Mom! I was enjoying the warm breeze. It feels amazing out here!"

Mom smiled at me as she walked towards the car to put her own bag in the back seat. "It's going to be a great night for a concert. We'd better get going, so we aren't late for dinner with the Cardinals."

I nodded before closing the door and plunking down into the passenger seat. I twisted to grab my seatbelt before Mom could slide into the driver's seat. She wouldn't take off before she checked I had the belt fastened. Mom settled behind the steering wheel and started the car, monitoring the gauges. After a few minutes, she pulled her own seatbelt and clicked it in place before looking at me. "All fastened in?"

I snapped the seatbelt and nodded. "Yup! Let's roll. I can't wait for dinner. I wonder what kinds of things Sam eats."

Mom put the car in reverse and backed out of the driveway, looking three times before she merged onto the road. Putting the car in drive, we headed to Sam's house. Zaps of excitement fluttered through my body, causing me to smile as the trees lining our road blurred by my window. Hope filled my soul that Mom and Sam would hit it off and become a couple. Butterflies flew in my stomach as I whispered a secret prayer to whatever god was listening for Maria and me to hit it off as well.

Chapter 3

We pulled up to the address Sam had given us, 15 Shady Grove Lane. Sam wasn't kidding when he said it was close to the river. His house sat up on a high cliff with a walkway winding down to the river below. I scrambled out of the car and ran to the edge of the iron fence to peer down.

"Tempy, be careful!" Mom called after me when she realized where I was headed.

I looked over the edge. Taking note, they fenced in the yard to prevent someone from falling down a thirty-foot embankment. A chill ran through me as the cool air from the water blew over me. I turned around to find Mom waving, but she wasn't waving at me. Walking back towards the car, Sam stood on the porch next to a girl.

"Hello!" Sam bellowed while he waved before descending the stairs to walk towards Mom. He reached her side and held out his hands to take the bags she had slung over her shoulder.

Sam and Mom talked before he led her towards the guest house he'd mentioned the other day. I looked up at the porch where the young woman stood staring down at me. Her hair was as black as the dress she wore. Locking eyes with her, I swallowed. This was the moment of truth. She stood there for a minute before she smiled.

"Hello, I'm Maria. You must be Tempest."

I exhaled the breath I had been holding when she spoke. "Hi, Maria. You can call me Tempy. I'm glad to finally meet you."

Maria smiled and motioned for me to come to the porch. "Why don't you come in and help me set the table for dinner."

Nodding, I smiled as I made my way up the four steps and onto the porch. I followed Maria through the screen door and into the home's entrance. The walls had to be at least ten feet tall. I let out a small gasp when I looked up at the ceiling. A chandelier decorated with thousands of crystals hung from the middle. Maria's laugh drew my gaze back to her.

"Pretty extravagant for an appliance sales guy, right?"

I held up my hands and shook my head. "I didn't mean to presume anything. I'm sure your dad does well with his sales."

Maria doubled over at my statement and let out a roar of a laugh. It bounced off the walls. "It's OK, I'm not offended. This house has been in my family since they first built the home. It's actually on the historic registry and we have to keep most of the house looking like a scene from the 1800's. If it were up to me, I'd gut the place and modernize it, but I'm sure you've learned that isn't how it works here in this town."

I let the tension fall out of my shoulders and gave Maria a smile. "Ain't that the truth! This place is definitely different from the town I lived in before."

"Where did you live before?" Maria asked as she continued walking through the house.

I followed Maria, continuing to talk with her. "Until about five years ago, we lived in New York. After my grandmother died, my mom needed a change. She somehow discovered the storefront she bought for sale online and moved us here. I still don't know how she found this town. I mean, it barely shows up on an internet search despite it being the capital of a state."

"That's crazy! I couldn't imagine leaving somewhere exciting like New York to come here. Maybe your mom knew somebody who lived down here? Like a relative?"

I shook my head and shrugged. "No clue. Mom's a very private person when it comes to stuff like that."

Maria stopped in front of a cabinet and grabbed a stack of plates. She turned around and cocked her eyebrow at me. "Your mom doesn't talk about your other relatives?"

"No, not really. Her mom was the grandmother we stayed with in New York, so I assume she's at least from New York. But I don't have a clue about my dad. For all I know, he could be from here."

Maria's expression fell into a frown. "You don't talk to your dad?"

I laughed and shook my head. "He died when I was two, so no, I don't talk to my dad."

Maria gasped as she clamped her hand over her mouth.

"It's OK. I don't really remember him. It's not a touchy subject with me, but it is for my mom, so I don't press it."

"Wow, that's a mature outlook on things. I'm still not over my mom's death." Tears formed at the corner of Maria's eyes as she blinked while handing the plates to me.

I took the plates and plastered on a smile hoping to save the mood from turning sour. "So, what's for dinner?"

"Pizza, spaghetti, garlic sticks, and salad."

My mouth fell open. "Are you serious? My mom's a baker and we don't have spreads like that at home!"

"Yeah, dad wasn't sure what to feed you all. We haven't entertained for a few years. He figured in the very least we could eat the pizza tomorrow for lunch if you all got full."

I licked my lips. "Mmm! I love leftover pizza."

"Me too! I especially love cold pizza for breakfast."

I smiled as I sat out the plates around the circular dining table. Voices carried down the hallway as Sam and Mom came into the house. I heard the front door shutting before they both appeared in the doorway of the dining room.

Sam smiled when he saw Maria and me working to get the table set. "Ah good, you two appear to be getting along fine in here. I hope you all are hungry. We have quite the feast this evening."

"Sam, I hope you didn't go to too much trouble for me and Tempy. We aren't picky eaters."

Maria shook her head. "I assure you, Miss Danvers, dinner was no trouble at all. We can eat the leftovers tomorrow for lunch."

Mom nodded and started towards a chair, but before she could pull it out, Sam stopped her.

Sam smiled a big, cheesy grin as he pulled out the chair for Mom. He bowed, holding his hand towards the chair. "My lady, allow me to assist you with your seat."

Mom giggled before sliding into the chair and allowing Sam to push her up to the table. "Thank you, kind sir."

I stood there rolling my eyes, but secretly smiled at the two. They were both goofy, and I hoped this was the beginning of a new start for them. Turning, I smiled at Maria, who also smirked as she watched the pair. I reached out and touched her elbow. "Maria, let's grab the food so these two can keep acting like goobers."

Maria laughed as she nodded. "Sounds good to me. I'm starved."

AFTER DINNER, SAM AND Mom headed towards the amphitheater, opting to walk down the path along the riverbank. It surprised me when Mom agreed, given it was pitch black outside, but I took it as a sign she was comfortable around Sam.

I helped Maria put away the leftovers and wash our dirty plates before following her into the sitting room. Instead of finding the Victorian era furniture I pictured, a matching set of oversized leather furniture greeted us as we entered the room. Massive, built-in bookshelves lined one wall and a giant fireplace stood along the farthest wall.

Maria flopped down on a large couch before looking at me. "So, what do you want to do? If you want to watch cheesy Halloween movies on TV, we can go to the guest house. We don't have cable in

14

the main house because plaster walls don't like TV cables. Or if you are a book nerd, you can sit in here and read books."

I looked at the books and then back at the girl on the sofa. "Something tells me you don't want to read books?"

"Yeah, I find it extremely boring. I only read when I have to for class. I have an eidetic memory and once I've read a book, I've read a book. I gotta keep my brain empty for more important things."

I smirked. "What's more important than information from books?"

Maria jumped up and flung her arms wide open. "Fashion, dear!"

Cocking my head, I raised a brow. "What is interesting about fashion? I mean, it's not like you are memorizing a chemical equation to make clothes."

"Oh, but that is where you are wrong! To be a fashion designer, you must constantly analyze your competition, watch trends, and if you want a real edge, you have to eyeball your clientele and size their clothes on the fly."

I shook my head at the description while scrunching up my nose. "Sounds fast paced and mind-boggling."

"It can be, but I plan on going to a fashion design school to help me learn all the ins and outs I don't already know."

"You already have your future planned out? I thought your dad said you were seventeen?"

"I am, but a girl can dream! The college I want to get into is a design school in New York. It's the same one my mom went to. It's hard to get accepted at the school, but being a legacy and having some stellar grades from another college before I apply will help. Don't you know what you want to do when you grow up?"

I rubbed my arms and took in a deep breath. Whenever I mentioned my goals to other kids, they usually laughed. I wanted Maria and us to be friends, especially if Mom and Sam hit it off, but it was painfully clear we were quite different. "I'd like to be an author. You know, write boring books."

Maria smiled. "Just because I don't like reading books doesn't mean I'd laugh at your vocational dreams, Tempy."

I looked up, letting out the breath I didn't even realize I held. "Well, that's not the response I usually receive."

"What does your mom think of your chosen career? Is she mad you don't want to bake?"

I laughed. "No, but we don't ever talk about stuff like that. She said she would support whatever career I wanted to attempt. I'm afraid to tell her what I am interested in writing, though. I don't want it to upset her."

Maria frowned. "Why would what you write upset your mom? Unless you want to write smut books and she's a big Bible thumper or something?"

Snickering, I shook my head. "No, it's nothing like that. I want to write murder mystery novels."

Maria squinted her eyes at me and opened her mouth, but shut it again.

"My dad was a cop, and an antsy robber gunned him down. He wasn't on duty when he died. I'm afraid if I told my mom the kinds of things I research to write, it would send her into a tailspin of anxiety and guilt. What I'd like to do is get a degree in forensic science to help me write more authentic works, but I'm sure my mom fears me following in my dad's footsteps. So, I don't talk to her about any of this. I have no desire to be a cop, but it's hard to write a murder-mystery for a contemporary audience when all you have to rely on is Agatha Christie novels."

Maria nodded before resting her chin on her fist. She looked towards the fireplace, staring off into the distance. "What are your feelings about a Ouija board?"

"Uhm, not sure I follow you on that one."

"What if we used the Ouija board to reach out to your dad and ask him some questions about how best to write your books?"

I looked at my watch. Mom and Sam wouldn't be back for another two hours. I shrugged. "I don't think the dead speak, but sure, why not? As long as we are done before our parents come back. I wouldn't want to upset Mom."

Chapter 4

"Great, come on! My stuff is in the guest house in my room." Maria charged out the door before I could ask any other questions.

I chased after Maria, but a gnawing feeling twisted in the pit of my stomach. Mom expected me to be in the main house. What if she got back, and I wasn't there? "Should we leave a note for our parents about being in the guest house?"

Maria stopped in her tracks and spun around. "Yeah, lemme grab my key and we can lock the main house up. I'll leave a note on the fridge. My dad always looks there to see where I am headed."

I stood on the front porch, waiting, as Maria dashed back inside. I looked up at the sky as a cool breeze blew over me. The temperature had dropped more than I was used to. Probably because of the water. Goose bumps rose on my arms, causing me to rub them. A loud bang caused me to jump. I turned to find Maria, letting the screen door slam behind me.

"Sorry! I need to oil the hinges on this old door, so it doesn't slam when I let go. I grabbed us some popcorn from the pantry while I was in there. There's a fridge in my room that's full of soda. Let's go!"

I followed Maria across the lawn and up to the main entrance of the guest house. While not as large as the main house, the structure was bigger than a breadbox. Maria inserted her key into the door before flinging it open. The lights automatically came on with the movement. Following her in and shutting the door behind us, I turned around, amazed. The front room was bigger than my entire house. "You call this a guest house? This place is like an entire house!"

Maria laughed as she bolted the door and armed the alarm. "Yeah, this used to be a carriage house, but a fire swept through the building a few years ago when a wayward firework landed on the roof. There was no saving the structure. My parents got permission to rebuild this into a modern structure, given the old one was beyond repair. Well, I guess their lawyer really did most of the convincing. Anyway, my mom had these plans for a house she wanted to build. She designed them herself. Before she got sick, my parents planned on building the house of her dreams in another town. Dad ended up building it here instead. Most of the time I stay here because, well, cable."

Spinning around, I took in the grandeur of the open floor plan. They equipped the kitchen with stainless steel appliances. In the middle of the area stood a granite countertop. "Wow, my mom would flip out at this kitchen. Of course, I wouldn't expect an appliance man to have crappy appliances."

"Yeah, I prefer cooking in here over cooking in the main house. I swear the stove hates me. Plus, this house has a dishwasher. My room's upstairs."

Maria led the way up the stairs, turning left and going down a hallway, stopping in front of a deep purple door. When she flicked on the light in her room, it surprised me to find light lavender walls instead of the gray or black I had imagined. The layout of her room was more like a mini-hotel suite than anything. She had a bed, a couch, and a large table all neatly laid out in the space.

"I think I understand why you prefer to live here instead of in the main house."

Rummaging in her closet, I heard only a faint laugh as Maria looked for what I assumed was her Ouija board. Maria spun around with something in her hand a moment later, shutting the closet door with her foot. She walked towards the square table off to the side of her room, depositing the board in the middle of the tabletop. "Here it is! Truth be told, I don't believe in this much. Maybe that's why it never worked for me?"

I walked to the table and pulled out the chair closest to me. I eyed the Ouija board. "I never believed in these either, but it sure does seem fun. We can try a few times and then watch a movie?"

"Sure! Let me grab the pointer doohicky thingy."

I couldn't hold back my snicker. "Doohicky thingy? I think it's called a planchette."

Maria shrugged. "Eh, you know what I mean."

Maria retrieved the planchette and placed it on the board before pulling out a piece of paper with what appeared to be pre-printed instructions.

"OK, it says to place the doohicky pointy thingy here and then we each take a side. Then we clear our minds and ask the spirit world to commune with us."

Nodding, I followed Maria's lead and placed my right pointer finger on the side of the planchette closest to me. I closed my eyes and took in a deep breath. I wasn't sure what to say. So, I drew inspiration from every cheesy movie I ever saw where they worked with a spirit board. "Great and magical spirits. Please let us know you are here."

I sat with my eyes closed for a moment before the board moved under my fingers. My eyes flew open as I figured Maria was messing with me. "Are you doing that?"

Maria shook her head and let go of the planchette. "No, I've never had this thing respond in the slightest."

We both watched as the planchette zipped around the board of its own volition. The board moved over the letters H-E-L-L-O. A breath caught in my throat. "Well, this has been fun, but how about watching a movie now?"

Maria nodded and quickly stuffed the board back into the box she pulled it from. She ran over to the closet and threw the box in, slamming the door behind her. Her eyes remained large as saucers. I noticed her hand shook as she grabbed the TV remote and began flipping through the channels for something to watch. She stopped on a channel promising a zombie marathon.

"You good with zombies?"

"Yup. You ready for soda and popcorn?"

Maria jumped up and ran to her small fridge. She brought back two canned drinks, along with her scavenged popcorn bag. "Do you want a blanket in case you fall asleep?"

Setting my drink down on a coaster in front of me, I nodded. "Yes, I have a bad habit of falling asleep when trying to watch anything at night. That's why I go to movies in the middle of the day!"

Maria walked to another closet on the wall opposite to the one she pulled her Ouija board out from. She returned with two fluffy steel-colored blankets and handed me one. "The bathroom is across the hall if you fall asleep and find yourself disoriented."

I unfolded the soft blanket and snuggled into the couch, munching on caramel popcorn and drinking soda. I remember finishing my snacks right before an epic zombie invasion, but after that I must have fallen asleep because everything went black.

I don't typically have dreams at night, but when I do, they're often weird. This time I found myself standing in a pitch-black room with nothing but an overhead lamp like you'd find in one of those old gum shoe movies. I remember looking around, wondering what was going on, when a voice spoke to me.

"Hello, Tempest. I am glad you stopped by to visit me. Just look at you! You've grown into a fine young lady."

I turned to find a man sitting under the lamp in a comfy chair. His brown hair and green eyes seemed familiar, but other than that, I wasn't sure who this man was. "Uhm, I'm sorry... have we met?"

The man smiled. "We met a long time ago. You probably don't remember me at all. You were so young when I had to leave. I see your grandmother's gift hasn't skipped you after all. Your mom and I argued over whether we should tell you about Gamma Tempest. I take it by the look on your face, your mom decided not to tell you much of anything."

I squinted my eyes as my heart started pounding in my chest. "Dad?"

"In the flesh. Er, well, I guess, ether? Maybe gaseous state? Never mind. Yes, I'm your father!"

"I don't understand. How am I talking to you?"

"Your friend forgot to close the gateway you all opened with the board. For a normal person, it wouldn't matter much. But for you, being around an open portal for hours has jolted your metaphysical powers awake."

I took a step back. This was even weirder than my normal weird. "My powers?"

"My family has a rich history of having women with supernatural powers and gifts. Your Gamma Tempest, your namesake, was what some would call a witch."

I grabbed my arm and pinched, but I didn't wake up.

"Sorry kiddo, that won't work. You aren't dreaming. It's more like your spirit has traveled through a portal to the Otherland and you're having a conversation with me. You'll need to go back through the portal to leave."

Sweat beaded down my forehead as my body turned clammy. I was going to have an all-out panic attack. Was I trapped here?

"Breathe, honey. You can leave here when you're ready. All you have to do is touch me. But before you bolt out of here on me, is there anything you want to ask me?"

That's right! Maria had wanted to help me write books by asking my dad for help. But somehow that didn't feel right. "Is there some way I can help Mom move on from the trauma of your death?"

Dad nodded as a sad smile crossed his lips. "Sometimes I visit your mom when she sleeps. I feel the weight hanging on her heart over my death. I've tried to help her the best I can, but she never believes me when she meets me here."

"Woah, what?! Mom can travel to this realm too?"

"A determined soul can do a lot. I am determined to watch over my family, and your mom is hell bent on healing. She was a different person before I died. I think she can find that person again, but it's the guilt holding her down in misery."

"So, what can I do if you can't help her? I was two when you died. I've only ever known mom as she is now."

"Your mom wrote me a poem once when she thought it was better for us to break up. We had different dreams, and she didn't see how our relationship could work. She didn't want me to feel guilty, but she also didn't want to let me go. She never showed the poem to anyone but me, and when we got back together, I burned the letter and told her no regrets. I think if you tell her this poem, she might listen."

I nodded. "I'll try anything to help her."

"Follow me, my love, to your demise, follow me, my love, to the next sunrise. I know you'd follow me anywhere I asked, but what was is now past. Follow your heart to your dreams. Follow your path along the glittering sun beams. I won't be a rock around your neck. I won't be the death of your light. Forget about me and disappear into the night. I want you to dance in your new life."

Tears ran down my cheeks as the beauty of the words hit me. "And you think when I tell her this, she'll be better? It's such a sad poem."

"Tell her the poem and then tell her I need her to dance in her new life. To let go of the rock around her neck."

"Alright, I will take your message to her. Now what?"

"Morning is coming fast. You need to return to your plane of existence. Come, give your old man a hug so you can skedaddle."

I walked towards the familiar green eyes I remembered from the picture of my dad hanging on the living room wall. I leaned down and wrapped my arms around his neck. Even though this was some kind of weird dream or alternative dimension, I could feel his arms wrap around me. All kinds of feelings welled up inside of me as I blurted out a last farewell. "I love you, Dad."

Bolting up from whatever happened to me, I found myself in an unfamiliar bed. Rolling over, I found my mom asleep on the other side. I rubbed my head, trying to make heads or tails of what happened. Was it a weird dream? If I recite the poem to my mom, will she go off the deep end? I blew out a breath and prayed I could figure out the best thing to say.

Mom rolled over a minute later, opening her eyes. They locked on me and formed a scowl.

"Are you alright, Tempy?"

I put on my best smile. "Yeah, I had a weird dream. Probably the late-night soda and popcorn fest. Did you have a nice time?"

Sitting up, Mom bit her lower lip. "I did have a nice time. Sam invited me out again next weekend, but I turned him down."

"Mom! Why would you turn him down? Sam's a nice guy. You will never be happy if you keep turning the men folk down."

Mom's shoulders slumped as she rested her face in her hands. "Please, Tempy, don't make this any harder than it needs to be. I know you had an enjoyable time with Maria and all, but I'm not ready for this."

I gritted my teeth, watching my mom commit relationship suicide. "Mom, listen to me. You can't blame yourself forever for Dad's death. It's been over ten years now and you deserve to have a life. You deserve to have a boyfriend. What are you going to do when I leave, and your nest is empty?"

Mom patted my leg. "You're young Tempy, and I'm sure everything seems crystal clear to you, but life is complicated and messy. I can't drag Sam into my mess. It wouldn't be fair. I'm a broken old lady with nothing to offer."

"Listen to yourself! I don't think Sam would have asked you out or bent over backwards to accommodate your fears about me being left alone if he didn't understand your quirks. Don't ruin this relationship before you've tried."

"It would be better if Sam and I parted ways, Tempy. Our dreams don't match up and I don't want to be a rock around his neck."

Those words bore down into my very being. They were almost what Dad had said she said to him when she tried to break up with him. The words came falling out of my mouth before I could stop them. "You said something similar to Dad when you tried to dump him. Are you afraid of commitment?"

Her mouth fell open as she gasped. "How did you know I said something like that to your father?"

"Because I dreamed about him last night. He told me about how you tried to dump him and the poem you wrote. He told me to tell you he needs you to dance in your new life and to let go of the rock around your neck!"

A look of terror washed over Mom's face. "Tempy, I never want you to talk about this dream again, OK?"

My brows knitted together as I frowned. Mom never wanted me to find out about Gamma Tempest and her gifts, but my dream was proof I found out about these mystical powers despite what Mom wanted. But I wasn't letting her off that easily. I was going to use this situation to my advantage for the both of us. "Fine, I'll never mention this again if you do as Dad asked. Can you let go of the guilt and try to give Sam a chance?"

Tears welled up in her eyes as she nodded. "I guess I could use a little more happiness, huh?"

I smiled back at my mom, satisfied I reached her. "You deserve happiness, Mom."

I FELT LIKE I HAD REACHED a turning point that day. Mom gave Sam a chance, and it wasn't long before she was Mrs. Cardinal. For so long, Mom and I had lived under a cloud of sadness, but it seemed to me like the sun was finally shining on me. Maria and I became inseparable sisters over the years. We moved into the guest house full time to give our parents privacy. I almost forgot what it was like to be sad, but happiness is such a fleeting character in the play of life, often disappearing when you least expect it.

I kept true to my promise, and I never spoke to anyone about the dream of my dad after that night. After seeing the look of panic on my mother's face, I figured it would be easier to ignore any magical powers I might have. I just wish someone had told the ghosts I wasn't interested.

Chapter 5: 10 Years Later

"Thank you for joining us today, Miss Danvers. I can't tell you how excited I am to interview you about your best-selling books! Can you give our audience an idea of where these stories come from? You're not a cop, but most of your details make every book you publish look like a walk through an actual crime scene."

Through the video chat window, I smiled at Carmilla de Langeu. "I'd love to say there was a secret method to my madness, but there really isn't. I spent years reading mystery novels and watching crime shows. I've also read many of the crime scene reports available to the public. Mix all of that in with my imagination and my brain cooks up a wild ride."

"You sure cook up wild rides! Your latest book is a riveting story about a young man murdered by a jealous co-worker. Of course, one can't help noticing the similarities between the murder of Josiah Wright and your fictional character Robert Collywobbles. How do you address those critics who say you prey off salacious murders for money?"

I smirked as I shook my head. "People will draw lines anywhere they can. Do my books have similarities to famous murders? Of course, but I'm basing my stories off human nature. If you look hard enough, you will find similarities in many murder cases. Anything from motive to execution. However, I'd like to point out many of the details of my books are drastically different from the actual crimes they're compared to. If I were simply waiting for a headlining murder to come along to plagiarize, I don't think I could get as many books out as I do. I write fast, but not that fast!"

Carmilla clapped. "Thank you, love. That's all the time we have today for this episode. Be sure to follow Miss Danvers on her social media accounts for a chance to win her new book, *Jealousy Loves A Promotion*."

I sat holding my smile until the screen gave the all-clear signal. I waited for Carmilla to turn back around and speak to me.

"Whew! Thanks for answering those tough questions, doll face. I love how you always come on my show and keep it real. I can't wait to see your next book. You'll send me an ARC copy, right?" Carmilla waggled her eyebrow at me as she smiled.

"Thank you so much for inviting me back for this book's launch. I'd be more than happy to send a preview of the next one to your address on file. It should be ready in a few months."

I air kissed the screen, all the while keeping my fake smile plastered on until Carmilla disappeared. I powered off my computer and placed the camera's protective cover over the lens. Standing up, I stretched before grabbing the purple wig off my head and placing it back on the empty wig stand. Being a famous person who values privacy is hard, but lucky for me, my adoring fans never see the real me. Most fans are content when I appear on the occasional talk show and then forget about me again until I have a new book available. Of course, I take precautions and alter my physical appearance anytime the author Tempest Danvers is out and about. In fact, outside of my family, no one has any idea my hair is brown nor that my true eye color is a brilliant, and sometimes odd looking, light green. I also take great care to cover my identity so I can avoid any doxing issues. My publisher and agent take care of most of the fine details. Although, I'm still not fully sure how anyone keeps me hidden, especially since I use my real name, but somehow, the company pulls it off.

I wandered out of my office, closing the door behind me. I rolled my shoulders, allowing the tension to ease out of them before pulling out my color contacts and placing them in their case. Finally, I flopped down on the couch in the sitting room in a pile of exhaustion. Laying there, listening to the sound of nothing, I drifted off to sleep when my doorbell rang. Moaning, I sat up and moved towards the peep hole. A young man with blue-black hair and a peculiar shade of amber eyes stood waiting at my door. I hesitated before opening the door a crack.

"Yes, may I help you?"

The man grimaced at me, blowing a mosquito away from his face. He didn't look any happier to be on my porch than I did to have him on my porch. "Are you Tempest Danvers?"

I fidgeted from one foot to the other, but kept the door cracked, trying to brace myself should he attempt to force his way into the house. "Uh, yeah, who are you?"

"I'm Detective Jax Dupree from NYPD. I've been tasked with delivering this package to you."

I raised my brow at the stranger. "Why would a NYPD detective be on my porch in the middle of Kentucky with a package?"

"Look, lady, I get it's weird, but I have this package from our evidence locker. My commanding officer asked me to bring this to you personally. I have business in these parts, and I wasn't given an option of declining this errand. Just take it so I can be on my way."

I shook my head. "No, that's OK. You can leave it on the porch. I'll grab it later."

The man sighed before looking down at the porch. "It's something from your stepsister's personal effects. Since her case is closed, we have to return the property."

Anger boiled through me as I opened the door wider. "You mean since you all gave up on finding who killed my sister and ruled it a sloppy suicide, you want to make room in your stores for somebody else's stuff so you can fail the next family?"

Jax took a step back and raised his hands. "Look, I'm doing as my CO asked. I'll put this envelope here on this chair and you can decide when you pick it up, OK?"

Flinging the door open all the way now, I gritted my teeth as I held out my hand. "Give it to me and leave my property."

"Gladly," Jax said as he dropped the padded envelope into my outstretched hand. He smirked at me as he released the package.

I snatched the envelope before whirling around and slamming the door in detective jackass's face. I turned the parcel over in my hands, finding the pull tab. When I was angry, none of my anxiety surfaced. I didn't hesitate to shake the contents out into my waiting palm. When the cold metal hit my flesh, my knees buckled. I slid down the door and onto the floor, holding my prize. Sunlight glinted off my sister's necklace. Under the fancy shirt I wore for the interview, I had a matching one hanging from my neck. A golden peapod where the peas were our birthstones. Our parents thought it was funny to give us something to remember the two peas in a pod we used to be.

I choked on tears as I stroked the blue sapphire of her pea set next to the blood red ruby of mine. "Maria, I know it's been a year, but I don't believe for one minute you committed suicide. I know Mom and Dad don't buy that story either. For all my supposed super sleuthing powers, I couldn't figure out how you were murdered. It's days like this I feel the impostor syndrome the most. Maybe those haters are right. I cannibalize sensational stories from the headlines and profit off them."

I closed my hands over the charm and held the trinket close to my heart. Tears escaped my eyes before I let the sobs wrack out of my chest. "I wish I could talk to you again, Maria. Why did you have to leave me?"

Tears soaked through my shirt as snot ran down my lips. I hadn't had a pity party in several months. Mrs. Ansel was proud of how much I'd recovered since my sister's death, but today was a disappointment. I sat on the floor crying, not able to move, just like I had the day I found out she was gone. I needed to move, but my body felt so heavy with grief I couldn't stand. Of course, what happened next should have been no surprise, at least not for me.

"Why are you sitting on the floor crying, Tempy? We have work to do. I always thought your stories were more memoirs than murder mysteries, and now I know why."

I raised my gaze to meet the eyes of the person speaking. "If you knew, why did it take you so long to come to me, Maria?"

"Because my soul is bound to my necklace, and I can't manifest away from it."

I gasped at the words. "How is that possible?"

"Of all the things to surprise you, ghost talker, the fact I am bound to an object shocks you?"

I closed my eyes and leaned my head back against the door, letting out a sigh. The sigh turned into a laugh. "No, I guess it shouldn't surprise me. So, what do you need me to do to help you move on?"

"Dismantle an organized crime ring and take my killer to jail."

"Is that all? Sounds like a typical Tuesday to me."

Maria fidgeted around.

It was fun to watch a ghost, a supernatural being, showing trepidation.

"There's more."

I crossed my arms and raised my brow towards my sister. "Well, go on, out with it then."

"Demons. Demons run the crime ring."

I giggled as I climbed to a standing position. "OK, well, maybe not a typical Tuesday. Where do we start?"

Maria smiled. Even as a ghost, her smile filled the room and commanded attention. "I tell you my story."

I nodded before walking back towards my office to prepare for the most important writing session in my life. Today, I was going to help find the person who murdered my sister.

Chapter 6

Sitting down at my desk, I picked up my favorite pen and notebook. I took in a deep breath and nodded before looking at my sister. "Alright, let's start from the top, Maria."

Maria smirked. "I was born in a small town down by the river."

I flopped my head back and let out a laugh. "Even in death, your sense of humor is bad. Now, stop being silly and tell me the good parts of the story."

"My name is Maria Cardinal, and Julian Devereaux murdered me. Although all official reports have ruled my death a suicide, just another young success succumbing to the vices of their career; I'd like the record to reflect the story is, in fact, a load of bullshit."

"Wow, that's an interesting intro, Sis. Do you have any kind of proof I can use? Where do I start? I obviously can't waltz into Julian Deveraux's office and demand to speak to him."

"No, you can't go near Julian. He's a bad guy, and he'd hurt you. Remember how I said he was a demon? Well, it wasn't a metaphor."

Pausing, I looked up at Maria. "What do you mean by demon? Like a Halloween demon story? Devil demon?"

"I mean the non-humankind. It doesn't matter if Julian is human or not. If we can get enough evidence to prove he murdered me, a human jail will hold him."

"OK, but again, where am I going to find this evidence? I don't solve crimes. I only pretend like I do in my books."

"The dirty cop Julian had on his payroll switched my real autopsy and crime scene reports with phony ones. He took the actual reports and hid them in his apartment on West 36th Street."

I stopped writing and raised my eyebrow. "You mean this dirty cop lived in the same area you did? How could a cop afford to live there?"

"Even better, the guy lived in the same building as me. I'm sure Julian owns the building and a perk of being a dirty cop is living the high life in a fancy art déco warehouse turned apartment building."

I clasped the back of my neck with my hand as I stared down at the paper. The words dirty cop stuck out like a sore thumb. "Do you know this cop's name?"

"I only heard Julian order Jax to come down there and clean this up. I think I was still in shock from the murder and not quite used to my ghostly senses yet. Other than that, I don't know much about this cop."

I gritted my teeth as my stomach continued to lurch. "Did this cop have a weird shade of amber eyes? Maybe blue-black hair?"

Maria flickered before dropping her mouth open. "How would you know that?"

"I think your dirty cop was the one who delivered you to me an hour ago. He said his name was Jax Dupree from the NYPD and he had the most memorable shade of amber eyes I've ever seen. But wait, why didn't you know he brought you here?"

"I think there was something in the envelope preventing me from being conscious. From the bits and pieces I remember from the night of my murder, I know Julian screamed at Jax to burn my necklace. I don't know why, but instead of burning the necklace, he packed me around in his shirt pocket for a few days. That's how I know he swapped out the reports and covered up the real paper trail. Then, at some point, he shoved me into a padded envelope. After he closed the package, all I could sense was darkness lulling me into a dreamlike state. Now, since I am no longer in the package, I am more aware, like I had started to become before he shoved me into the envelope."

Rubbing my hands over my face, I let out a sigh. "I'm sorry, Maria. You shouldn't have had to suffer for so long. If I had only known you were in the evidence bin all this time, I would have come for you myself."

"Don't sweat it, Sis. Those were some boring ass days being in limbo, but it's all good now. I'm home and you are going to help me break up an international demon crime ring, yeah?"

A pang of sadness ran over me. She was still her optimistic self, even in death. "Maria, do you know what day it is?"

"No, I think it was September 10th a few days ago. You know I've never been good with timeframes."

A tear escaped from my eye and ran down my cheek. My poor sister had no idea she'd been gone a year. How do you break something like that to a ghost? Most of the departed I meet have a grasp on time. "Maria, today is October 30th."

"Oh, wow, hum. I've been dead for like a month now? I guess being in the envelope messed with my senses."

I bit my lip before speaking, staring at my hands resting on my lap. Summoning the courage to tell Maria the truth, I looked up into her eyes. "You've been gone for more than a year now, Maria."

Maria's face fell as she pursed her lips. "A year?"

"Yeah, they told us you died on September 12th. We went to New York as a family and claimed your body. Julian and Dad got into a big fight over where you were going to be buried. Julian didn't want your body to come back here to Kentucky, but Dad has some scary lawyers. We didn't know when we took your body part of you was stuck in New York."

"Julian was always an overprotective ass when it came to me. I don't understand how he could kill me. We were engaged, for crying out loud. He told me he was in love with me. I was a stupid fool to ever fall into bed with him."

I shook my head while I twirled my pen in my fingers. "Do you have any idea why Julian killed you?"

"No, my memory of the attack is hazy. I'm not sure if that's normal or whatever for a person killed in a traumatic way, but I'm hoping it will come back to me."

"If your memory doesn't come back, how am I supposed to help put Julian in jail?"

Maria started pacing back and forth across the room. "I'm sure if we could procure the true autopsy report and the police report, we could build a case. Prove I wasn't a suicide. Hopefully, there will be enough to point a finger and have Julian investigated."

"OK, let's say for now the reports are key. How are we going to obtain them?"

Maria smiled. "Break into a dirty cop's fancy apartment when he's not home?"

"Maria, have you forgotten what my job is? I talk to ghosts and write books. I am not an armed criminal. How do you suggest I break into an apartment, let alone a dirty cop's apartment? We don't know if the reports are still hidden. You've lost a full year of time since he stashed them. Maybe he destroyed them."

Maria shrugged. "I hadn't gotten that far into the plot yet and the whole being dead a year thing really throws a wrench in the works. I think if we stake out Mr. Dirty Cop's apartment, we can see when he leaves and how long he's gone. Then, we can make a move when we know more information. You can break in, go to the spot I tell you, then run out. Easy peasy."

I rolled my eyes while shaking my head. "You've watched too many episodes of *Crime Report*. We can't stake out a cop's house.

Besides, I already know he isn't in New York because he is down this way doing business. That's why he brought your necklace to me."

Maria clapped her ghost hands together and jumped up and down. "Which means if we leave ASAP we can break in and be gone before he comes back!"

"Except we don't know how long he's going to be away."

"Which is why we have to leave now!"

"I can't pick up and go to New York with no explanation."

"Then don't. Tell your mom what you are doing."

"She'd have a coronary if she thought I was speaking to ghosts again."

Maria shrugged, throwing her ghost hands up into the air. "Then lie about wanting to honor my memory by going to fashion week at the Independent Pineapple."

I let out a groan. "I hate the Independent Pineapple,"

"It's a perfect cover story. We get in, we get out, and you don't have to go to the Pineapple."

I shook my head. "I don't think our parents would buy that story. But maybe if I say I'm going to New York for a month or so to help write my next book?"

Maria frowned. "Would Mom seriously buy into you living in New York for a month to write a book?"

"It's not typical for me, but if I spin it right, I can say going to New York would be great for me, both personally and professionally. Besides, it's not like anyone can stop me from going. I am an adult."

Maria let out a laugh. "I think my angle would convince Mom, but you do whatever. Just find a way for us to travel to New York ASAP!"

I ran my fingers through my hair and nodded. "I'll call my agent in the morning to see if she can arrange for me to look at some space to rent. A hotel would be too conspicuous. For now, I'm headed to bed."

Falling down into my bed, I didn't even bother taking off my fancy shirt. Pulling the covers over my head, I drifted off to sleep with one thing on my mind. *What in the world did I agree to?*

Chapter 7

I stood listening to the agent drone on and on about the features of the apartment we were walking through. She was too bubbly and excited to be showing THE Tempest Danvers a short-term apartment.

"Over here we have a lovely sleeping area hidden behind this free-standing room within a room. And if you open this little area's door, you will find a stellar writing nook. Plus, the roof terrace is to die for. All of this is within walking distance to the Independent Pineapple, and most of the fashion shows this week." Jane squealed as she waved her hands in front of her body.

I took in a deep breath before pressing my fingers to my temples. "And how much for a month in this complex?"

Jane flipped open her padded leather notebook to look at some numbers before nodding and looking back up at me. "Since it's a sub-lease, and it's Fashion Week, we couldn't possibly take less than $10,000 payable today."

I had to pick my mouth up off the floor. I figured rent was expensive in New York, but I didn't expect to buy a new car for the property owner. "Look, Jane, this is a great place and all, but I don't have ten grand to drop on a rental for a month. I may be a bestselling author, but I can buy two cars and a horse where I come from for that kind of money."

Jane snapped her leather notebook closed before pursing her lips. "I see, well I thought you realized how expensive Manhattan living is, even if it is temporary. Could your publisher provide you with some more money for living expenses? Your agent said you wanted to capture the true ambiance of living in New York."

"Yeah, no, that's not how my publisher works. I have to cover all my expenses up front and then I am reimbursed a small percentage at the end of the year. It's OK. I'll rent a room for a few days, do some people watching at local cafes, and soak in all the ambiance I can on a budget of a thousand dollars or less."

Jane scrunched up her nose. "You'll never be able to capture what it's like to live in New York on a three-day tour."

I held up my hand. "It'll be enough for me to form an idea. The best part of being a fiction writer is I don't have to get everything right. Artistic license is real in my line of work."

"Alright, I understand. I'm sorry I couldn't be of more help. But, since we didn't close a deal today, do you think you could give me your autograph and maybe clue me into what this new book will be about?"

Smiling, I nodded at the young woman. "I'll be glad to give you a personalized autograph as a thank you for your help today. But, as for my next book, I've only come up with a working title. I'm thinking of calling it *Silenced by Suicide: Murder in Loft 36*. It'll be up to my publisher if they like the title or not, but it helps me with my save files!"

Jane's eyes bugged out of her head as her face blanched. "Did you say Loft 36?"

"Yeah, but that's the part I'm not sure my publisher will like. I don't usually include numbers in my titles."

Jane fidgeted with her notebook clasp. "Where did you come up with that loft number?"

I shrugged. "No idea. The number popped into my head one day."

Jane flipped open her notebook again, turning a few pages while muttering to herself. She shook her head, cursing under her breath.

She finally stopped and looked up from her book of listings. "I wasn't going to mention this one apartment because something bad happened there, but you are a horror writer of sorts, and it is an odd coincidence the number is Loft 36. I don't know how comfortable you would be there."

Throwing my hands out in front of me, I shrugged. "Well, you've piqued my interest. Spit it out already!"

"I have one loft not unlike this one in a building two buildings down. The loft is supposedly haunted because the last resident killed herself. Rumor has it, the young lady was under a lot of pressure and trying to make it as a fashion designer. It's a sad story and though it's been more than a year, I can't find anyone to stay in the place. If you were interested in renting an unusual space like this, I could probably make the rental agreement for a full month for only twenty-five hundred dollars. The building owner is quite wealthy, so he doesn't care, but my rental agency does care because it's like a blemish on our company. I think if we could rent the space out to someone with a lot of social media clout who spoke positively about the residence, we could probably rent the place out again at top dollar. Especially if you agree to tell your social media audience the apartment was a lovely place to stay and absolutely not haunted."

My chest tightened as I listened to Jane speak. I didn't have to know the address because I already knew where the loft would be. Memories of high-rise ceilings decorated in hammered tin art déco motifs adorning the space flashed through my mind. Although I had never stood there, I remembered the balcony overlooked a lovely garden, and the kitchen had all stainless-steel appliances. I knew because Jane was talking about Maria. Loft 36 wasn't something I pulled out of thin air; it was Maria's loft number. "Hey, that sounds like a perfect place for me. Let's go!"

Jane's smile beamed across her face. "Follow me! We can leave the car here and walk."

I waited until Jane turned around to make a face. Maria giggled at my side. She remembered I hated walking almost as much as large crowds. Thank goodness I didn't like wearing heels. After a day of space hunting and a bonus walking tour of the road, I was going to feel the burn tomorrow.

Maria bounced next to me. "You know what this means?"

I checked to make sure Jane wasn't looking before shrugging. I didn't need the real estate lady to think I was bonkers.

Maria's eyes lit up as she rubbed her hands in glee. "The dirty cop lives in the building. We can break in while he is away, and it will be much less conspicuous. No staking anything out trying to play a game of chicken. We could do the job tonight if you swing this deal."

We stopped in front of the entrance to the onetime warehouse, turned into chic luxury lofts. The building reached for the sky and looked like it never ended. An eerie feeling of being watched washed over me. Unease fluttered through my stomach. I bit my lip before deciding to probe Jane. "Hey, Jane. If we can make a deal on this rental, can you assure me of my privacy? I don't mind taking lots of promotional pictures and releasing them once I'm gone, but this is my first time staying in a place like Manhattan."

Jane turned on her toes to face me before placing a hand on my shoulder. "Oh, honey, don't worry. Other than this one poor soul who killed herself, this building is safe. Don't let the history of the place being a warehouse fool you. The owner uses the finest high-tech security available on the market today. Plus, I'll let you in on a little secret. One neighbor, a man who is, by the way, H-A-W-T, is a police officer. He's only two doors up in Loft 34 and I am sure he'd love to serve and protect a cute girl like yourself. Know what I mean?"

I eked out a smile on Jane's face, but the thought of me doing anything other than breaking into this guy's apartment made me want to spew. As soon as she turned around, I made the universal gag me sign to Maria. I couldn't wait for this misadventure to be over. I reluctantly followed Jane through the revolving door and into the main lobby. A large wooden desk sat on the left side of the lobby, while two golden elevators occupied the middle of the room. A set of marble stairs stood hidden away towards the right. Growing tired of looking like a blundering idiot on her first trip to a big city, I walked over to Jane, who was talking to a man behind the wooden desk.

"Maurice, I am here to show Loft 36. Can you give me the usual pass? I have a great feeling we may finally rent the place."

The man Jane called Maurice stood in front of a computer, never looking up at her. He tapped on keys while making unhappy noises. Finally, he stopped and looked straight at me before giving me a disapproving grimace. "Have you vetted this one, Jane? She doesn't seem like she has the money for a luxury loft in the premier facility we have here. She has purple hair, after all."

"She checks out just fine, Maurice. Remember, it's my job to rent the spaces while you greet the tenants. Not act as if you are put off by doing your job or showing disdain for the clients. So, cut me some slack here. I'm sure my friend is tired after our day of house hunting and would like to possibly rent the space ASAP."

Maurice smirked again before producing a plastic card and handing it to Jane. "If she rents the place, I'll need ID before she gets one of these and a copy of the signed lease agreement. I'd have Jax vet her as well, but he is away for yet another week on a business trip."

Jane rolled her eyes. "Maurice, I know the drill. I've rented out almost all of floor six myself over the last several years. I hope your day gets better and if my friend here rents the place, please don't be such a grump."

A slight smile flashed across Maurice's lips before his face went blank again. I waited until we were in the elevator before asking Jane more about Maurice.

"So, are you friends with the Maurice guy, or what?"

"Not quite. Maurice has made it clear to me on more than one occasion his desire to court me, if you will. I don't want to ruin a working relationship or complicate my job by fraternizing with an important contact at a rental facility."

I raised my brow. "What's with the medieval speak there? Court? Who courts?

"Dating always sounded so neanderthal to me. I like to call it courting. Using the term reminds me of courtly love and ancient romance. I want something grander than dating. I'm sure Maurice is the type who can offer me the swooping romance I desire, but I don't think I'm ready to accept such a relationship. Besides, I've been hooking up with the cute night manager after hours for a few months now. He's a graduate student working his way through his final year, and I've been helping him with his thesis on sexual surrogacy therapy."

"Wait, the night manager is a prostitute?"

"No, he's going to be a sex therapist and is writing his thesis paper on different techniques for sexual surrogacy. I met Jonathan here during a late-night tour with a client and we got to talking. I found him quite humorous, especially when he brought up his need for a sexual research partner. He made a joke about how finding a partner for his thesis wasn't really something he could advertise for in the paper. I was curious about the deal, so I asked him some more questions. Before I knew it, I had agreed to be his testing partner. Sure, I may be waiting for a grand romance, but that doesn't mean having no-strings attached sex in the name of science is out. Sadly, he's going to be done with his paper here in a few weeks. We're scheduled to meet tonight after work for his last experiment on orgasm prolongation."

My eyes bugged out of my head and my jaw hit the floor when I realized what Jane said. "Why are you telling me all of this? Isn't this a little too much information for someone you met today?"

"Jonathan has made me realize we need to be more forward about sex and stop hiding it in the closet like it's a shameful thing to do. We should talk about sex like we would about going to the gym. A lot of our sexual dysfunction comes from our learned shame of the act."

The elevator stopped and dinged before the doors opened into a sea of deep crimson carpet. A golden wallpaper accented by silver leaves lined the walls. We turned left out of the elevator and walked a few feet down the hallway before coming to a large window. Sunlight pouring through the glass illuminated the number on the door we stood close to. A golden 34 beckoned to me like a moth to a flame.

Jane paused before pointing to the door while fanning herself. "This is where Mr. McHottie Cop lives. Man, what I wouldn't do to sign up for a ride on his cruiser, preferably while handcuffed."

The statement sounded off to me causing me to grimace. "Uh, did you mean in his cruiser? And why would you want to be handcuffed? Do you want to be arrested? Is that on your bucket list or something?"

Jane barked out a loud laugh. "No, silly, I was trying to tone down my sex talk by using a euphemism. Based on your reaction to my disclosure in the elevator, I figured your head might explode if I came right out and yelled I wanted the hot cop to handcuff me to his bed so he could give me a good pounding."

After the shock of Jane's confession wore off, I made a mental note of where the dirty cop's loft was in comparison to the elevator. I wouldn't have much time to pick a lock, not that I knew how to, but I didn't need to waste any time stumbling down the hallway lost trying to find the right door.

Jane and I continued down the hallway before stopping in front of Loft 36. I watched as she slid the key card through a contraption on the door causing a light to flash before the lock on the door released.

With a swooping motion, Jane flung the door open. "Well, here we are! This apartment comes fully furnished and if you feel like cooking, we have several excellent delivery services for groceries. You literally never have to leave this room your entire time here."

I sucked in a deep breath before crossing the threshold of my dead sister's apartment. A cool breeze wafted through the air like having a window open on an early spring day. My gaze wandered around the living space I remembered so well from my sister's video calls. I knew why the apartment was furnished, too. These items were the things Dad refused to bring back with us when we came here to claim Maria's body. She had been so proud of the space she decorated, and Sam just couldn't bear to take all her hard work back only to stuff the items into storage. He had hoped the next person would appreciate Maria's efforts. Tears pricked my eyes. "This is a lovely space, Jane. The ambiance of New York oozes through every crevice."

"I am so glad you are happy with the place. I can make a call to my manager to draw up the paperwork, including a clause to share your time here for a reduced rate."

I nodded, pretending to spin and take in my surroundings, turning instead to wipe a wayward tear from my eye. While spinning, an idea came to my mind, which might further help me in my attempts to gain access to Loft 34. I stopped spinning and looked at my real estate guide. "Yes, the sooner I can settle in, the better. One quick question, though. I saw you using the card to enter this loft. How safe is the system? I've read about hackers copying key cards."

"Not these! I assure you those are stories from places with poor tech. The systems may all look alike, but the one here sports topline encryption. If it helps, I'll also give you this copy of the key card so you can have it before I leave. Other than the one Maurice makes you, and of course, the master card at the front desk, no one will come in here without your invitation. On top of that, there is a deadbolt, which only works from the inside. You can lock the deadbolt while you are in your apartment and not even someone with a keycard can enter while the bolt is engaged. But seriously, this complex is secure."

"Well, I guess you had better print those papers for me to sign!"

Jane dialed a number on her phone before walking off towards the door. "Mirela! Good news, I have a fabulous offer on Loft 36. Can you fax me over the standard clause for one month plus the celebrity discount page? No, I can't tell you who is staying here. At least not until they are done with the space."

I hung back as Jane went to collect the fax from her boss. Maria appeared on my right side and stared at the floor in front of the fireplace.

"What's wrong, Maria?"

"Nothing. What could be wrong? I'm dead. What more do I have to worry about?"

I sucked in a deep breath when I saw the spot she focused on. I knew from the limited report we received from the NYPD they found Maria's body right there in front of the fireplace on her faux white fur carpet. I walked closer to where Maria stood. I clenched my fists together, not knowing how to comfort her.

"I promise you, Sis, some way I'm going to prove you were murdered. I have a few days to figure some things out, but I will get into Loft 34."

Chapter 8

I sat on the couch in my newly acquired loft, tapping away on my laptop, looking for clues on how to break and enter into a high-tech secured home. At least as a writer, I could research things like this and say it was all for a book. Of course, private search mode also helped hide my trail. It was well past midnight, and my eyes drooped with the need for sleep. I shut the lid before flopping back on the couch. I had almost fallen asleep when Maria started talking.

"Why are you asleep? This is no time to rest. We are on a limited timetable to break into the cop's apartment."

I opened my eyes, not offering to sit back up. "You've been dead for a bit, Sis, so I'll give you a pass, but if you remember us folks still walking around in meat suits have to sleep."

Maria stomped her foot, but it made no sound. "Fine, take your beauty sleep. I'm going to explore and see what I can find. Don't sleep on the couch. You know how much your neck will hurt if you do."

I smiled as Maria flickered out of the room. It was amazing to me how much she was like the Maria I remember. Realizing this gave me a small flutter of happiness because it meant all the ghosts I had ever talked to before weren't simply putting on a good show for me in the personality department. Which also meant the night I met my father, he was acting like he did in life. I stood up from the couch, deposited my laptop onto the coffee table, and made my way around to the bedroom. Unlike the apartment we looked at earlier in the day, this loft had actual walls and no weird cube rooms. Whoever remodeled this warehouse took care to make sure every inch of space was expertly crafted and would command a high rental value for years to come.

Shirking my shoes, shirt, and pants at the bedroom door, I grabbed for my travel bag sitting on the chest of drawers. I laid my wig carefully on the dresser to keep the hair from getting too mussed. Running my fingers through my dark brown hair, I massaged my scalp. The wig was the highest quality, but being stuck wearing one all day still made my head ache. I was glad I opted to wear oversized sunglasses and leave the colored contacts in their case during my house hunting adventure.

I dug around in my bag to find my flannel pajama bottoms. Pulling them on, I opted to pair them with my camisole. For an old, drafty warehouse, this building had surprising heat retention, and I knew the matching flannel top would be too much once I crawled under the blankets. For a split second, I wondered if they had washed these sheets in the last year. However, my brain decided sleep was more pressing. I fell asleep only seconds after my head hit the pillow. I'm not sure how long I got to sleep before Maria appeared next to the bed and started talking a mile a minute.

"Tempy! I found someone who can help us. Tempy! Wake up!"

I opened one eye and squinted at my sister. "For the love of all which is holy, what do you want now, Maria?"

"I said I found somebody who could help us with the break in job!"

I let out a sigh. "Who did you find?"

The question left my lips at the same time as I saw Maria waving towards the doorway. I raised my brow when the form of a man appeared standing in the room. The appearance of the man didn't frighten me, but rather puzzled me. I looked at Maria and then at the man.

"Tempy, this is Hector. I met him on the fourth floor. It surprised him to run into another spirit wandering around the building and after chatting for a bit, he has offered to help us in our quest."

I sat up in bed, staring at Maria. "How exactly is Hector here going to help us and, for that matter, why would he help us?"

Maria crossed her arms. "Tempy, don't be rude, the man is standing right there. Ask him yourself."

Groaning, I rubbed the sleep out of my eyes. "Hello, Hector, it's nice to meet you. Can you tell me exactly how and why you can help with our predicament?"

The man, unlike the other spirits I spoke to, flickered in and out of my sight. "I want to help you because Julian killed me in this building. Julian is a bad guy, and I don't think I can rest until he's paid for his crimes. I'll do whatever I still can to help you."

"OK, so tell me what you think you can do? I appreciate the offer, but both you and my sister are non-corporeal. It's not like you can break into the loft for me."

Hector's brow furrowed before he blinked out of the room and then back into view. "I can give you tips on how to re-write the key cards to open any door in here."

"I thought this place had high-tech security?"

Hector shook his head. "No, this place hasn't changed security packages in the last ten years. They tell you it's safe, but they haven't bothered with any of the updates. They think since the technology in this building is scarce, the chances of finding someone who can break into the place is worth the gamble of not upgrading."

"And you're sure you can help me sneak into Loft 34?"

"Yeah, lady; if getting you into Loft 34 helps take Julian down so I can rest, I'm all for it. I've been gone for almost eleven years and I'm tired of being trapped here. It's easy to break into the lofts. You just need an RFID chip encoder and a laptop."

I wrinkled my brow and bit my lip. "And where exactly would I procure one of those?"

"Black market, but sometimes you can get them at office supply stores."

I rolled my eyes while groaning. "Oh, OK, I'll just go down to the front desk and ask for the way to the nearest black market for my illegal goods."

"Sis, shush. Hector is going to help us. The least you can do is a search on the web and try to find one of those doodads. A lot has changed in ten years. We can probably have one of those thingies ready to ship to us in a few minutes."

"Fine!" I flipped the covers off my body and trudged back to the table where I left my laptop. I pulled open the lid and typed in RFID chip encoders. Both Maria and Hector stood behind me, looking over my shoulder. The search showed nearly a dozen models available for purchase and shipping. I had no idea what I was looking for.

"Which one should I buy?"

"Any of them will do, ma'am."

I scanned the page of choices before deciding on one which would arrive in a few days. "OK, looks like we can have this here by Wednesday. Can you come back on Wednesday, Hector?"

The ghost shrugged before flickering. "I don't know. Maybe if Maria shows me how to find you again."

I spun around to face Hector. "What do you mean if Maria shows you how to find me again? Can't you home in on me or whatever specters do to find people?"

"No, ma'am. I may be a jilted specter, but I'm a class two entity. I need a go-between, like your sister Maria, to reach out to a living being. It's hard to explain, but some spirits are weaker than others. Your sister is a powerful class five, and she can reach out to the living on her own. Other spirits aren't so lucky."

"You mean there are spirits out there who can't reach people like me?"

"Yeah, and for those of us who can't communicate with the living or pass on to the afterlife, it's a lonely existence. I think this is what they must have meant by limbo. Maybe I should have paid more attention in church."

I shook my head. "I'm sorry, Hector. I had no idea there were spirits who couldn't communicate with anyone. Maybe if you hang around my room until the part arrives, it won't be as hard to find me again."

"OK, I'll stay around here where Maria can find me." Hector's head hung low as his form faded from the room.

"Hey, Hector, wait a moment. You said you couldn't rest until Julian went down for your murder, right? Well, do you have a story you want me to tell the world?"

"No, ma'am. There isn't much of a story for me to tell. I was a low-level bad guy who got on the wrong side of a high-level bad guy. Once Julian got what he wanted from me, he did away with me. The police found my body, but my reputation didn't warrant anyone caring. I turned up dead. They did the minimal investigation needed and slapped my file into a cold case bin. Meanwhile, Julian is out there living his best life, doing whatever he wants."

"If you are such a weak entity, how do you know your case went into a cold case bin? Can you travel away from this building?"

"I'm tied to this property, but Julian has cops in his pocket. Some of 'em even live here, and they talk shop."

I gulped at the thought of more dirty cops living in this building. "How many cops live here in this building, and do you know which lofts?"

"They rotate around from time to time staying here when Julian tells 'em to stay. I only know of one who lives here all the time, and his name is Jax. He's a high-ranking player in Julian's court of bad guys."

"Great! And here I am trying to break into a high-ranking dirty cop's apartment. Look, Hector, I may not have the skills to pull this heist off, but I'm going to do my best to make Julian pay for his crimes."

Hector shrugged. "You're the only hope I've had in the last eleven years I've been stuck wandering this building. I don't have a choice but to believe you will be anything other than successful."

With those parting words, Hector flickered out of my view. A lump formed in my throat. I had my work cut out for me and not a lot of support. "Maria, I'm going back to bed. If you happen to find any more friends to help us, don't wake me up before noon."

Chapter 9

The key card fizzled and popped inside the chip reader. Waving the smoke away, I frowned. "Is it supposed to do that, Hector?"

Hector's form blinked before shrugging. "Sometimes you pick up a bad card, and the reader melts the chip. Sometimes the reader is bad. It's not an exact science, ma'am."

"Well, I only have one spare card. What should I do?"

Maria twirled around the room. "We should try the second card just to be sure."

"And if it doesn't work?"

Maria rolled her eyes. "Duh! We find a way to obtain another keycard and try again."

Leaning back on the couch, I rubbed my hands over my eyes. I hadn't slept well since Maria introduced me to Hector because I couldn't shake the idea of someone watching me. I hadn't left the loft since the first night and the only people who could get in were never around when the unease struck. "Maybe I'm not cut out for this. I've obviously messed up this simple key hack. I could have a hundred of these plastic keys and probably still mess them all up."

Maria sat down next to me. She reached out her hand to touch my shoulder, but her hand went through my body instead. A cold pain shot down my arm, causing me to grimace.

Maria's head hung low at my reaction. "Sorry, I forgot I can't touch stuff."

"It's OK, Sis. I know you meant well. Hector, what do I do once the reader turns green?"

"You can take the card out and try it on a door."

I leaned forward and tapped the button on my laptop's screen to start the software working on encoding the spare card before leaning back on the couch. With any luck, I would soon have my master key card, or I would have two broken key cards and need to come up with an excuse to come by another one or six. The little machine made a whizzing noise, but thankfully no popping this time. I kept an eye on the percentage bar as it trudged towards and finally reached the ninety-nine-percentage mark. I held my breath, praying the other 1% would finish without a hitch. After a few seconds, which seemed like an eternity, the computer dinged with success. I let out my breath as I grabbed the card and held it up for inspection. "So, this card will now open any of the doors in the building and no one can trace the activity back to me, right?"

Hector shook his head. "No, ma'am. If anyone looks, the access records will only log a master key card code."

"OK, then let's find out if the card works. Maria and Hector, I need you two to stand point out in the hallway and let me know when the coast is clear. Heck, walk through the apartments and check out the occupants and let me know if anyone might catch me coming or going from the loft."

"No problem, Sis. Hector can go stand in the hallway and I'll make a lap through all the apartments up here. I'll be right back."

Maria vanished through my wall, followed by Hector, while I stood waiting in the middle of the apartment's living room. After a few moments, Maria's head appeared through my door.

"Come on, Tempy, most people are at work right now. The cop's not in his room either, but I looked at his calendar and saw today's date circled, so I think he might come back tonight. It's now or never."

Taking in a deep breath, I steeled my nerves for what I needed to do next. I, Tempest Danvers, Best Selling Author, was going to

55

break into a dirty cop's apartment with a makeshift master keycard I made with the help of a ruffian ghost. This was going to be like an episode of *Supernatural* crossed with *COPS*. I grabbed the door handle before pushing myself outside into the hallway. Maria was nowhere to be seen, but across the way I noticed Hector standing guard. I nodded to him before walking down the hallway. Out of the corner of my eye, a brief blip of something shiny caught my attention, but when I stopped to look, the spot disappeared.

Maria reappeared in front of Loft 34 and waved. "Come on, Sis, we are under the wire here."

I moved down the hallway and stood in front of the door with the number 34. This was no time for hesitation. I raised the keycard and lifted my head in confidence, pretending I belonged there. After I swiped the card, I heard a small noise as the tumblers turned to disengage the lock. I turned the handle and barged through the doorway, shutting the door behind me as quickly as I could. "OK, Maria, what am I looking for?"

Maria chewed at her lip. "Well, I'm not sure."

Throwing up my arms, I yelled. "What! What do you mean? I'm standing here in a cop's apartment, and you don't know what I'm supposed to look for?"

"I was in his shirt pocket, remember?"

While suppressing a scream, I pulled my hair. I took a few deep breaths, trying to think how I could rectify this situation. "If you go back in the necklace and I pack your around, would it help?"

Maria shrugged. "It's worth a try."

"Great, zap back in the necklace and I'll put you under my shirt. That should be close to being in the pocket." I grabbed the chain of Maria's necklace and tucked it under my shirt. The pendants were easy to tell apart because her birthstone was at the top of her pea pod, while my necklace had the stones reversed in my pea pod.

After flipping the light on, I walked straight ahead. I wasn't sure which way to go, and Maria couldn't talk to me as well while she was in the pendant. I walked around the living room of the apartment, taking in the spartan style. Next to the far window stood a heavy wooden desk, but instead of the piles of paper you find on most people's tables, this one was empty. Something about the desk drew me to it, despite the emptiness. I walked around behind the desk and pulled out the chair before I could stop myself. Sitting down, I instinctively closed my eyes and inhaled deeply. Immediately, my nose filled with the scent of autumn leaves blowing on a fall day. In my mind, I saw an image develop. I saw Jax walk into the room with a stack of papers. He ran towards where I sat, but I didn't jolt out of the seat. Instead, he pulled a book from the shelf along the wall before flinging the tome down on the desk. He then moved to open the book, but instead of the inside being pages, the book was hollow. Jax put an envelope inside and closed the book before saying a funny word. The scene in my mind receded, leaving me dazed.

Standing, I turned and looked at the bookshelf. None of the books looked like what I saw in whatever I had just witnessed. Something moved off in the corner of my eye, something shiny like in the hallway, but when I turned to look, the light disappeared. Turning back, something compelled me to raise my hand and close my eyes. Using my will, for lack of a better description, I pushed my desire to find the book down through my fingers. When I opened my eyes, a bright light blinked on the spine of one book. Grabbing the illuminated volume from the shelf, I took it over to the desk. Laying the book down, I attempted to pull the cover open as Jax had. Unfortunately, my efforts were met with my hand receiving a shock.

I shook my hand as I yelped. "Ouch! What the hell? Is this book rigged to be electric?"

Maria manifested next to me. "What's wrong, Tempy?"

I shook my head and looked down at my foot. "I don't know. This book. I can't explain. You'll think I'm crazy."

"Says the ghost to her sister. You know the sister who can talk to ghosts. Who am I to judge you? Tell me what happened."

"A vision drew me to this desk and when I sat down, I saw I guess a memory. I don't know what else to call it. But Jax came in here and hid something in this book. None of the books on the shelf right now looked like they did in the vision, but when I stretched out my hand, I somehow willed this book to make itself known. I'm pretty sure, since this one is glowing, I need to open it, but the book shocked me when I tried."

Maria's face scrunched up. "Maybe it has a spell on it! Do you know any magic words?"

Flabbergasted, I turned to face Maria. "What makes you think I know magic?"

"I dunno, didn't your dad mention something about your Gamma Tempest having powers? Maybe you have powers. I mean, you talk to ghosts."

A laugh escaped my lips. "Oh, my goodness, Maria, being dead has made you more irrational!"

"Well, maybe there's a word like open says me or something."

I shook my head. "No, but Jax said a funny word when he closed it. I don't know, it was something that sounded like an apple sauce brand."

Maria raised an eyebrow. "Was it something like *mots magiques*?"

I took a step back because the words caught me off guard. "How in the world would you know that?"

Maria looked down at the ground. "It's literally French for magic words. I was learning French for a fashion show next year. Well, I guess I mean this year. Anyway, I remembered the words from some celebrity social media post. And yeah, it reminded me of applesauce too!"

Shaking my head, I held out my hand and said, "*mots magiques*". I thought nothing had happened, but then I heard a tiny clicking sound and the book cover popped open. Reaching down, I tapped the book cover quickly, trying to avoid a shock. When I wasn't zapped, I pulled the cover open all the way to find the envelope I'd seen Jax with. The yellow packet was blank except for a single handwritten word. I looked up at my sister and then back at the package. "Holy shit, Maria! This has your name on it."

Chapter 10

M y hands trembled as I read Maria's name over and over. This was really the package we came to get. I stood there, staring in disbelief at the entire ordeal. How did I, a law-abiding private citizen, break into a guy's apartment and find a hidden box?

"Tempy! Stop zoning out. We need to leave now."

Maria's yelling pulled me back into the present. My head snapped up to meet her gaze. "What's with the urgency?"

"Uhm, Hector said he saw Jax walk into the building a few minutes ago. We have to get out of here."

"Shit!" Grabbing the box and envelope I ran to the door and yanked the handle open just as the elevator dinged signaling someone was coming. Pulling the door shut, I looked for some place to hide. I'd never be able to walk calmly down the hallway acting like nothing was up, but the only place I knew to go besides my apartment was the elevator. I moved away from apartment 34, putting myself into the middle of the hallway. A male voice trailed down the hallway. Panic set in as I looked for a place to go.

"Tempy, you gotta move!" Maria whaled at me.

I sucked in a deep breath and forced my legs to walk towards my apartment, but at this rate, I would never make it inside. Something across the hallway caught my attention, like the flashing light I kept seeing and missing. This time, the light looked like sunlight glinting off a mirror. I watched the globes of light bounce around until they settled on a recess in the wall. Something told me to walk towards the light. As I got closer to the light, I realized the area was a darkened hallway. As creepy as the hallway looked, I figured getting caught by a dirty cop would be worse. I darted into the darkness and went back as far as I could before running into a wall. The hallway blocked my line of sight, but part of apartment 34's door remained visible. As the door swung open, a head of blue-black hair disappeared through the opening. Before calling for Maria, I counted to ten.

"I'm right here, Tempy. You should probably ditch that book somewhere in case you can't make it back to the apartment before Jax comes out."

"You think he's going to come back out?"

"Hector is in there watching him right now. He's going to report back to us in a moment if Jax is acting normal or if he suspects anything."

Pulling out my cell phone, I used my flashlight to look for some place I could stash the stolen book container. Maria was right. It would be less suspicious to be seen in the hallway empty handed. Turning around, I realized the hallway was more like one of those snack alcoves in office buildings, only this one didn't have any vending machines. I found a table in there; so, I unceremoniously stashed the book under the table. Grabbing the envelope, I folded it several times and stuffed it down into a cargo pocket on my thigh, securing it with a zipper. I took a few deep breaths to center myself while I waited for Hector to come out and report to us about Jax. After a few anxious moments, Hector came out and made a beeline for us.

Maria phased in front of me, blocking Hector from coming all the way into my hiding spot. "Woah, Hector, what's wrong? What took you so long in there?"

"I had to hide so he couldn't tell I was in there and then I had to wait until he got into the shower to leave."

"What do you mean wait so he couldn't see you? Hector, we're dead. Who's going to see us?"

Hector shook his head as he blinked in and out of visibility before gulping. "I think Jax sees ghosts. And I think he suspects someone has been messing in his apartment, but he hasn't figured out if anything is missing or if someone only came in there."

Maria crossed her arms. "What makes you think he knows someone was in there?"

"He kept breathing in deeply around the desk and acting weird. He was muttering fresh rain and roses and smiling."

"OK, that is definitely weird. But you said he's in the shower, right? I am going to make a mad dash to the apartment. Even the quickest of showers needs at least five minutes. I figure I have at least three to get back inside the apartment. You two need to take the long way around. Avoid him at all costs, especially you, Maria, OK? Go through the floor or something if you need to."

I stood up straight, squaring my shoulders before beginning my mad dash across the hallway and then down to door 36. I leaned up against the door, shaking as I fumbled for the key card in my back pocket. Relief washed over me as I gripped the plastic square. I wanted nothing more than to get into the room and pack my bags. I hated wasting the money on the rental fees, but there were zero chances I was going to stay here after I just burglarized a cop's home, even if it was in the name of justice. The indicator flashed red when I swiped the card. "Damn it, you stupid little card. Don't do this now!"

I continued to argue with the card reader for a good three minutes, but the light still flashed red. I was so engrossed with arguing with the electronics, I never heard the person coming up behind me. Instead, a strong smell of autumn leaves invaded my nose before a voice rumbled behind me.

"Excuse me, do you need some help?" The male voice asked.

I tried to avoid turning around because I got the sense I would meet a pair of amber eyes if I did. Instead, I focused on the reader and shook my head. "No, thank you. Me and my card reader are just having a bad day. I'm sure with a few more swipes and maybe a well-placed punch, the little fella will see it my way." Before I could say anything else, an arm reached across my shoulder to pull my hand off the key card.

"I insist. I wouldn't want my new neighbor to kick her door down this early in her stay. Besides, you might need your door to keep out all the vagrants roaming the halls at night around here."

The comment caught me off guard causing me to turn around. I looked up into the most mysterious amber eyes while raising a brow. "What?"

A smile broke out on his face. "I'm joking. My name is Jax and I live in loft 34. If it helps ease your mind, I'm a police officer. I try to look out for my neighbors, even if they are only staying here temporarily."

My stomach lurched at the comment. *Did he know who I was?* I pulled my hands together to stop them from shaking while plastering on a huge smile. "Uh, yeah. I'm sorry. What makes you think I'm not staying here permanently?"

"Oh, I'm sorry, it's fashion week around here and with the purple hair, I kind of guessed you were here to take part. Most people who live here on this floor are snowbirds who leave during the cold months and sublet their apartments. We have a high turnover of neighbors here, but since I live here most of the time, I can usually pick out the newbies."

I flashed another fake smile. "Yeah, makes perfect sense."

Jax's eyes twinkled as he wiggled the key card in the slot. The light turned from red to green and the handle finally clicked, allowing Jax to push and hold open the door. "Sometimes you have to wiggle the cards. You'll get used to it, but stop by and get another key card tomorrow morning."

Grasping the handle and wiggling past Jax, I tried to flash yet another fake smile. "I think that's a great idea. I'll definitely look into getting a new card tomorrow. Thank you again for your help. Goodnight, Jax."

Jax nodded his head, not letting go of the door. "No problem, miss. Uhm, what was your name?"

The knot in my stomach grew tighter. "Oh, silly me, where are my manners? My name is Evelyn Potts. I'm only staying for a few days to do a little research on fashion week."

"Well, it's nice to meet you, Evelyn. I hope you have a pleasant stay here in New York."

At this point, the fake smile felt like a permanent fixture on my face. I tried to minimize the small talk to get him to leave, but he just kept lingering. "Thank you, Jax. Have a nice evening."

Jax let go of the door and turned to leave, but stopped and spun around again. "Hey, Evelyn, I was wondering if you might like to visit one of the premier fashion week clubs. A lot of the big designers hang out there."

I shook my head while making a face. "No, sorry. I'm not much of a club person. I'm strictly here to watch a show at the Independent Pineapple. I don't need to get involved in anything else in this town."

Jax leaned in closer to me, allowing his fingers to brush lightly against mine. The contact gave my fingers a little jolt. I tried to hide my eyes widening at the shock, but I was sure he picked up on my reaction because he leaned in closer.

"I insist you accompany me tonight as a guest. I'm part owner of Club Oubliez. I think the experience will leave you enlightened."

"Sorry, I didn't pack club clothes. I'm afraid I'd only embarrass you with my lack of non-cargo pants."

Jax traced my finger, sending more jolts up into my hand. "You don't need to dress fancy. The club has a laid-back vibe, which is why all the designers come there to unwind. I'll pick you and your purple hair up at eight."

"Sure, sounds great. I'll be ready."

"Great, I promise you won't regret coming." Jax turned and walked back to his doorway.

Once Jax went back into his own apartment, I closed my door, turning the giant dead bolt. Something was off about Jax. I leaned my head against the door and took in several deep breaths before spinning around to head in and take a shower. No sooner than I had turned around, a strange woman appeared before me. I knew she was a ghost, but she didn't appear fully human. "Hello?"

The ghost smiled, although the smile didn't reach her brilliant green eyes. "Oh Tempy, I wish you wouldn't get involved with Jax."

The fact this ghost knew my name, saw me talking to Jax, and apparently knew him creeped me out a bit. I opened my mouth to speak, but I couldn't find the words to say anything.

The ghost held up her hand. "You do not need to say anything, Tempy. I assure you, I am not some old stalker. I came here to help you."

Still in shock, my mouth fell open. "Help me how?"

The ghost sighed before walking closer. "I am your Gamma Tempest."

Chapter 11

I stumbled backwards and looked at the strange woman in front of me. I never met my Gamma Tempest, so I couldn't be sure she was who she said. "Excuse me, what did you say?"

"Your father reached out to me and asked me to come help you. And by the looks of the exchange you just had with Jax, you need my help more than ever."

I opened my mouth to speak, but all I could do was stand there and stare. Out of all the ghosts I ever spoke to, this one was the only one to catch me off guard enough to leave me speechless. I inhaled again to speak just as Maria appeared next to the woman claiming to be my Gamma.

Maria paid no attention to the ghost she stood next to, instead she raised her brow at me. "Hey, Sis. What's up with the weird face?"

I looked at Maria and then at the woman and then back at Maria. "Uhm, can't you see the ghost next to you, Maria?"

Maria turned her head, looked around, and then shrugged. "Are you having a mental breakdown? There is no one here but you and me."

Shaking my head, I made my way over to the couch to sit down before resting my head on my hands. "OK. I must be going insane. I committed a crime and now I'm doing time by going crazy."

The strange ghost woman appeared in front of me. "No Tempy, you aren't going insane. I'm veiled. You are the only person, living or dead, who can sense me while I am here on this plane of existence."

"Fine. Let's say what you are telling me is the truth. What help do you think I need?"

"I am here to warn you away from people like Jax."

"And how do you know Jax? He's like maybe twenty-three and last I checked you died twenty-four years ago."

"My dearest heart, Jax is older than I am. Last I checked, he was two-hundred years old. I was only one-hundred and twelve when I died. By the time I came into existence, Jax was an old man. Do not be fooled by him so easily. Use your gifts to peer beyond the veil."

I squeezed the bridge of my nose. "It's times like these I wish ghosts could bring me food. Such a shame about the non-corporeal aspect of death."

Maria flickered closer to me, her face squished in confusion. "Uhm, Tempy?"

I looked up at my sister. "Yeah, Maria?"

"Is this what it's like to be in the room with you while you talk to a ghost?"

I shrugged. "I don't know what you're talking about."

"Only hearing one part of the conversation. It's, well, weird and rather disconcerting."

I exhaled. "Gamma Tempest, can you please include Maria in your veil or whatever you call it? I need her to be in the loop on this."

"I don't know, Tempy. Seeing me might shock her."

I laughed while throwing up my hands at the ridiculous concern. "Gamma, she's dead. I don't think you can cause her any other harm. Besides, her spirit is bound to this necklace; so, I know I can find her again should something happen."

"Alright."

Surprise coated Maria's face as Gamma shimmered in the spot she occupied.

Maria's mouth fell open as she looked at me. "Holy shit! There's a woman over there."

"Maria, meet my Gamma Tempest. She says she doesn't want me to spend any time with Jax."

"How do you know this is your Gamma Tempest? Didn't she pass before you turned one?"

"Very astute observation, young lady. I could be anyone." Gamma smiled and winked at Maria.

I shrugged. "True, she could be anyone, but something deep down tells me I can trust her."

Gamma smiled. "Maybe I was wrong to worry about you. Your latent powers appear to be working."

I lifted a brow. "My what?"

With those words, Maria threw up her hands and backed away. "I think you all need to be alone for this conversation. I'll be back later."

"Maria! You can't abandon me here."

"Sorry, Sis. This sounds like a heavy discussion, and I don't want to distract you."

Before I could say anything more, Maria disappeared through the floor.

Gamma Tempest smiled as she waited. "As I was trying to explain, you have Fae gifts. Your primary gift is obviously penetrating the veil between the realms of the living and the dead. However, your aura tells me you can use some magic as well. With proper training, you might be a powerful mage. It makes sense. My family hales from the Summer and Autumn Court Nobility. Mortal blood is less likely to dilute your Fae side."

I held up a hand. "Summer Court? You mean like fairies from movies?"

A twinkle glimmered in Gamma Tempest's eye. "Something like that, dear."

My mouth formed the letter W before I stopped, not sure what to ask.

Gemma Tempest put up her hands. "I know this information is a lot to take in, and I wish I had prepared you, but after your father passed, I figured you didn't need the additional burden of learning about your Fae blood."

I raised my brow at the mention of my father. "Did my dad know about this Fae blood?"

"He knew a few things, but I was trying to live a simple life back in those days. Your father and your grandfather didn't need all the Fae drama learning the full truth would bring."

I smirked. "But I do?"

"No, but you are about to invite Fae drama into your life if you keep crossing paths with Jax."

"I don't want to cross paths with him ever again. If I could, I'd pick up and leave right now. But I have a feeling if I skipped out on Jax, he'd find some way to hunt me down. I plan on meeting him and then hightailing it out of this town."

"Tempy, I know you wish to solve the mystery Maria's death, but I strongly suggest leaving this one alone."

Shaking my head, I crossed my arms. "No, I promised Maria I would bring her killer to justice."

"Tempest, if you pursue this promise, you will become engulfed in the Fae world. Are you prepared to deal with learning everything you thought you knew may not be true?"

"Someone already tore my world asunder when Maria died. What else could happen?"

"You could get sucked into the politics of the Summer and Winter Courts. Your skills are powerful enough to draw attention should the Fae discover your abilities."

"OK. I just won't talk to any Fae. So, thanks for stopping by Gamma, but I shouldn't learn anything else about the Fae so I can avoid being sucked into that world. Feel free to stop by and haunt me like a non-Fae grandmother if you'd like."

Gamma Tempest threw her head back. "Seriously, Tempy, why are you being so stubborn? I'm trying to help you. I want to keep you safe."

"I am being safe, Gamma! Before you showed up, I didn't know Fae were real. Now, I do, and you say that's a dangerous thing to know. So, why tell me?"

Gamma shrugged her shoulders. "Because I thought you'd respond well to reason, dear. However, since you seem to need a bit of prodding. Let me ask you this. When you spoke to Jax, what scent did you pick up from him?"

The question froze me in my tracks. How could she know?

"He smelled like autumn leaves on a fall day, didn't he? And the smell made you feel comforted and at home."

My mouth fell open before I could stop the expression. "How did you know?"

Gamma sighed. "Because of the curse on our family."

At those words, I doubled over in laughter. I held my sides, trying to stifle the laughter long enough to enunciate my words. "Now we're cursed. What is this, a comedy of errors or something?"

"How I envy you and your free will. I wish you'd reconsider going down this path, Tempy. Do you still intend to meet Jax?"

"Yes, I do. I did just break into his home to steal incriminating evidence. I need to know if he has any idea I was in his loft or if he was simply being neighborly. I think if I leave before I meet with him, it will only give him a reason to follow me. Either way, I'll be out of here tomorrow. Besides, this town is giving me bad vibes and I don't need to be here to work on Maria's case anymore."

Gamma Tempest's face fell. "I understand. After all, you are of my blood, and we are a stubborn lot. Which is how our family line found ourselves cursed."

"What is this supposed curse, anyway? How bad could it be?"

"Once upon a time, a Fae woman fell in love with a mortal man. Such a union was unheard of. To make matters worse, the Fae who fell in love with the mortal was betrothed to the King of the Summer Court. The Fae female, Kinara, rejected her pledge to King Oberon. Choosing a mortal man over a Fae, especially a king, was a huge slight to all of Fairy. Thus, King Oberon cursed all the daughters of House Autumn to fall inexplicably in love with the royals of the Summer Court. Of course, the curse can only work if the child is inside of Fairy."

"And you don't want me to go anywhere near Fairy or Fae folk so the curse can't trigger?"

"Exactly. I want you to retain your free will and not become some mindless woman devoted to a Fae simply because he smelled nice."

"You mean like leaves on an autumn day?"

"Yes, and the more time you spend with a royal Fae, the more those scents will appeal to you. Your Fae blood will tell you your true home is at the Court of Autumn and will want you to embrace things which come from there. The curse will compel you to return to Fairy, but if you do, you will be part of Fairy forever."

"What are you trying to tell me, Gamma? Is Jax a royal Fae?"

"I'm sorry, dear. The curse prevents me from giving you all the information you need. I can't tell you explicitly who is or who is not a Fae, let alone who is from a royal house, but if someone says you smell like fresh rain and roses, be wary of them."

71

Chapter 12

Rummaging through my suitcase, I looked for the most club like clothing I had brought with me. Although Jax told me the club had a laid-back atmosphere, the place obviously was going to be full of hipsters. And a hipster's definition of laid back was not on par with mine. "Ugh, why did I tell him I was covering fashion week? I will stick out like a sore thumb."

"I'll help you not stick out too bad, Sis. Lay out all your clothes and I will tell you what to wear."

I dumped the contents of my bag out onto the bed before assembling them into outfits. Once I had the shirts laid out with the tops, I motioned to Maria. "This is all I brought with me."

Maria studied the clothes. "Yikes! You weren't kidding when you said you didn't have any club clothes. I hope you don't go on TV in these outfits."

I rolled my eyes. "No, Maria, I go on TV like once a year and my stylist always sends me an outfit."

"Look, the only thing we can do this late in the game is for me to tell you what to buy at the store next door. I'm sure there will be something from last season on clearance, which will make you more credible at the club."

"I didn't really budget for a wardrobe change in the middle of act two."

"Please, you have more money than a small country in your bank account. You can afford a clearance designer dress to help uncover the murder of your beloved sister, right?"

I stomped my feet. "I hate shopping for dresses! You know fashion isn't my thing."

"Fine! No shopping. Surely, I can pair something together with what you brought." Maria paused for a second, scanning my three shirts and three pairs of cargo pants. I watched her make a face at them before spinning around. "Wait, I know what you can wear and it's already here!"

"A shirt and a pair of cargo pants?"

"Even better! I have a designer dress in my closet. It should fit you well enough for the night. Plus, it's a classic style that won't look dated, which will help keep your cover while you're in the club. A person interested in fashion wouldn't show up in last season's looks."

I let out a groan. I always hated Maria's taste in dresses. If it was classic style, it meant it was short and black. "Is the dress what I think it is?"

Maria snickered. "Probably, but it's your best shot. Come on, Sis, show off those curves. I mean, it's the least you can do to honor your dear, dead loved one, right?"

"Oh, my goodness, Maria, stop with the guilt trip!" Marching over to the closet, I twisted the knob, opening the small cubby Maria called a closet. Inside, I found several dresses hanging in pristine garment bags. I reached and pulled all the bags out, taking them over to the bed to lay them down so I could unzip the white bags. In the first bag, I found a bright red dress with ruffles. I grimaced at the color, but at least this one looked like the material offered coverage of the important parts. I reached inside when Maria yelled at me.

"No Tempy, not the grandma dress!"

"Why not? Isn't it a designer dress?"

Maria scoffed. "Yes, for old people! Not hip young journalists covering something at the Independent Pineapple."

"Then why in the world do you have this dress?" I asked as I crossed my arms over my chest.

"The designer, who was an old lady, gifted me the dress at the end of one of my fashion shows. It would have been rude for me not to accept the dress."

"But you wouldn't wear this thing. How is it rude to refuse a gift you won't wear?"

Maria looked down. "I was going to give the dress to Mom for her birthday. A designer doesn't always care if the person you give a garment to wears the outfit, especially if the person accepting the gift gives the item to a loved one to wear. However, openly refusing a gift of a garment from a higher profile designer is career sabotage."

I stopped and looked back at the outfit. "Mom would have loved this dress. I'll make sure she gets it as a gift." Zipping the bag back up, I placed it to the side. I grabbed another white bag, pulling the zipper to reveal a green beaded flapper dress.

"Looks like bag number three is the lucky winner. You don't want to wear a flapper dress to a club. It goes against all the fashion rules."

"Really, Maria, more rules? What's wrong with this one?"

"I never got to finish the beading the way I envisioned."

I lifted my gaze from the dress to my sister. "This one is the one you were trying to design when we were kids, isn't it? The one from your dream?"

"Yes, but I hardly had any time to work on the dress. When my designs started being noticed, my life became too full to do the things I enjoyed."

"Maria, why didn't you tell me you were miserable here? You could have come home."

"I wasn't miserable, Tempy. It...it's just things weren't going as I planned. Then I met Julian and things went further off course. He got me all these contracts, and I spent most of my time overseeing things to fulfill those orders. The longer I stayed here, the more I lost touch with why I came. Plus, getting involved in Julian's business is how I learned he was into something bad."

"Did you ever figure out what Julian was doing? You told me he was involved in some kind of crime ring?"

"I never fully uncovered what he was doing, but I know it involved sending shipments of my outfits to weird places. I remember I was starting to put two and two together, but I wasn't fully able to figure out anything before, well, before Julian killed me." Maria looked down while grasping her arm, hugging it close to her body.

"Hey, don't sweat it, Sis. We will get through tonight and then work on your case once we get home." I picked up the third garment bag and unzipped it to find exactly what I thought the dress was going to be—a little black dress. Although this one was not as tight as I had imagined and sported tasteful black satin accents.

"See, classic beauty dress perfect for dinner functions, interviews, and hipster clubs. The dress also pairs great with combat boots and ripped fishnet stockings."

I held the dress up to my body while tears threatened to stream down my face. "You bought this for me, didn't you?"

"Yeah, I knew you'd never buy something fancy like this dress for yourself. So, when I saw it at the store on the corner in the clearance bin, I picked it up for you. I thought in the very least you could wear it for Halloween. If you look in the bag's bottom, there's a spiked bracelet, a pair of distressed fishnets, and a black leather necklace to go with the dress. I didn't buy matching shoes because you always have some kind of black boot on hand."

Laughing, I pulled my new zippered boots out of the bag. I hadn't worn them yet, but this pair was more fantasy inspired than combat themed. But as my sister had predicted, they were black. "Was I always so predictable to you?"

"Yes! Now hurry and get dressed. You don't have a lot of time and I know it will take you at least ten minutes to get those stockings on the way you want them."

I shook my head as I dropped my pants before reaching for the stockings. "I need to stop being so predictable!"

"No Tempy, don't ever stop being you. You are perfect in every way, even in your predictability."

I laughed as the stockings slid up over my legs with ease. These were definitely not the type we had back home. The stocking material caressed my skin while the tops hugged my thighs perfectly. Little bows with a tiny rhinestone in the center of each one decorated the sides. I moved to slip my boots on next so I wouldn't snag the stockings to pieces. There was nothing worse than having a runner and I would hate to ruin the last gift my sister ever got me by destroying the stockings on the floor. Next, I stepped into the dress, relieved to find a side zipper I could easily close. Unlike the off the rack garments I was used to, these pieces seemed luxuriously tailored. I ran my hands up and down the dress a few times before I heard the doorbell ring.

"Enough feeling yourself up there, Tempy; it's Jax. You gotta get your wig on before you can answer the door."

Shaking myself out of the trance, I grabbed my wig while rushing to look into the mirror to make sure the hairpiece sat perfectly on my head. Before dashing over to the front door, a glint of silver around my neck caught my attention. "Shit! I can't let Jax see my necklaces!" The doorbell sounded again almost with an impatient tone.

"It's fine, Tempy. Just take them off and let him in before he breaks down the door. I'll be OK if you have to leave me here."

"But what if someone comes in here and takes your necklace? You can't project too far away from it, remember?"

The doorbell rang again, this time with a long ring.

I leaned out the bedroom door and yelled. "Coming!"

"We can figure it out in a minute. Just let Jax in and tell him to give you five, OK?"

I took a deep breath before I ran to the front door, pulling it open without looking. On the other side stood Jax in a dress shirt and black dress pants. The top of his shirt hung open, thanks to the first two buttons being left undone. Part of his chest teased out from under the material. I caught myself staring before I heard him clear his throat.

"Are you ready to go, or do you want to ogle me some more?"

I stepped back away from the door as I felt my face flush with heat. "Wait, what? I wasn't ogling you. Come in. I need about five more minutes to get ready. Just have a seat on the couch. I promise I won't be long."

I didn't give Jax a chance to answer before I jetted off back to the bedroom, closing the door behind me. My eyes bulged out of my head as I looked at Maria. She opened her mouth to speak, and I shook my head while holding out my hand. I looked in the mirror one more time, cursing the fact I forgot to put in my color contacts. Snatching the case, I slammed the tiny plastic discs into my eyes, turning them from the odd shade of green to the dark blue I normally sported. I hoped Jax didn't notice the sudden change in my eye color. Looking around the belongings on my bed, I pulled out my small travel wallet and dumped out the change. I scooped up my necklaces and plopped them inside the compartment before zipping them shut and walking out towards the door. "You stay in there, OK?"

Jax, turning his head, smiled. "I didn't plan on watching you get dressed."

"Uhm, what?"

"I heard you say for me to stay in here. I assure you; I have no ulterior motives tonight. I didn't come early to watch you through a peephole or anything."

My head tilted to the side as I stood there staring at Jax. "What?"

Jax held up his hands. "Nothing, Miss Potts. I was simply trying to make a joke. Apparently, we have very different humor. I apologize."

"Miss, who?" The words were out of my mouth before I could stop them. Damn it! How could I forget my alias?

"Oh, did you prefer I call you Evelyn? Since we are practically strangers, I wasn't sure if you would want me to address you formally."

I smiled and nodded. "Oh, yes, Evelyn is fine. Sorry for the confusion. I'm just not used to anyone speaking to me."

Jax raised his brow while holding out his arm. "Shall we then, Evelyn?"

Nodding, I took his offered arm and followed him out of the door. All the while, electricity shocked my hand where I had it wrapped around his arm. *What was going on?*

Chapter 13

After an uncomfortably quiet ride in Jax's very expensive black sports car, we stood before the doors of Club Oubliez. The doorway was nondescript except for the hand painted sign above the door, which even without a neon light appeared to glow, and the bouncer checking ID's. A modest line made up of a hip looking crowd wrapped down the sidewalk. They didn't seem to mind when Jax cut to the front of the line, ushering us inside ahead of them. Walking in, I realized the entire atmosphere of the club was rather chill and unlike anything I'd ever seen. Instead of pulse pounding music, classical tunes filled the air from a state-of-the-art sound system. All around, patrons sat at little tables sipping drinks reminiscent of an old school jazz club. For a moment, the glamour of the nightclub had me entranced, but I quickly came back to reality when Jax grabbed my hand.

"Come on, I'll take you to my VIP section. There's less distraction in there."

Blindly, I followed behind Jax, allowing him to lead me to a more secluded part of the club, all the while the hairs on the back of my neck stood up issuing their unheeded warning. The electricity pulsed through my hand where Jax held onto me, causing my whole body to tingle. By the time we reached the back of the club where the VIP section was located, my whole body hummed. Jax sat down on a small, circular couch and before I knew it, I was sitting right next to him, not caring I was closer to him than I originally wanted.

"So, tell me, Evelyn, what's a young girl like you doing here in this big city all by yourself?"

"I already told you I'm here to write a piece on the Independent Pineapple show. After I finish the article, I'm headed back home for a well-deserved rest."

"What show are you interested in doing an article on?" Jax smiled as he wrapped his hand around mine once again.

The tingling shooting through my hand made it hard to concentrate. I tried to get my brain to work. I had looked up the schedule at the IP so I could answer questions, but the more Jax held my hand, the less I could think of words. "Uhm, the last one of the season. It has great potential."

"Interesting, so you will stay until Friday?" Jax squeezed my hand more.

Damn it, why couldn't I think? "No, I have to leave first thing tomorrow morning. I've already seen the show I needed to."

Jax smirked. "Really? Wow, you must be a grade A magic user then."

"Huh?"

"The event was so large this year, they extended the shows until Friday. The grand finale won't be until late Friday night."

"Oh, well, what a shame. I guess I'll have to miss that part of the show. They dated my plane ticket for tomorrow."

"I wouldn't think an aspiring fashion journalist would give up so easily. You know they can change plane tickets, right?"

"I do; however, I have other engagements I need to get back home to attend."

A grin broke out across Jax's face. "Interesting, but I thought you said you were going home for a rest after this?"

I felt my brows pull together in a scowl. "What exactly are we doing here, Jax? Did you bring me here to play twenty questions?"

"I'm simply doing my due diligence in vetting a new neighbor."

I pulled my hand away from Jax's grasp before crossing my arms. "Do you interrogate every recent visitor to your fine building?"

A laugh erupted from his chest. "Only the mysterious, pretty neighbors who make the rental company sign an NDA."

"Look, Jax, I don't know what you were hoping to find out about me, but I'm leaving tomorrow morning. So, don't worry about the enigma which is my life. I'll be out of your hair by tomorrow afternoon."

Jax sat back, eyeing me. "Somehow, I doubt that, Miss Potts. Or should I say, Tempest Danvers?"

I squinted my eyes and shrugged my shoulders. "I don't understand what you are talking about, Jax."

Jax leaned over and took a deep breath. "Just as I thought, fresh rain and roses. I knew I should have never brought you that damned necklace. Now look at you, following me around like a lost puppy. Breaking into my house and leaving your scent all over my place. And I bet you don't know why you are doing all of this, do you?"

Those words broke me out of whatever trance I had been under. Of course, he hadn't admitted to knowing anything of substance, like the fact I had Maria's packet of papers, but I wanted to see what other information I could get out of him. "So, you know?"

Jax reached his hand out to trace my face, stopping to rub his thumb on my lips. "Maurice had me run a background check on you before I got back into town. I know you're both Tempest Danvers, the author and Tempest Danvers, sister to the late Maria Cardinal. You have quite the security wall up around your identities. Whoever hides your identity is doing a top job. You should commend them."

I rolled my eyes as I let out a scoff. "Or maybe fire them. You broke the security around my identity?"

"What can I say, Miss Danvers? I'm one of the NYPD's finest detectives. Don't worry, most people will never get through the security around your split identity despite you boldly choosing to use your real name in both instances."

"So why drag me here to play twenty questions if you had the answers all along?"

Jax sat back before downing a shot of something in a glass I hadn't noticed before. "I asked you here because I couldn't risk the chance of you running away before I could confirm my theory about you."

Looking up into Jax's amber eyes, I froze like a deer caught in the headlights. The scent of autumn leaves and wind invaded my nose, causing my train of thoughts to fall away like water in a sieve. I pulled back a little from Jax, which allowed me to move away from the intoxicating scent just enough to regain some thoughts. "You have a theory about me?"

He leaned in closer until his lips were inches from mine. Raising his hand, he cupped the back of my head as his gaze pierced my very soul. "You're one of the missing Daughters of House Autumn hidden outside the land of Fairy."

I sucked in a breath, feeling a cool wind tickle my exposed skin. I fought hard to clear my thoughts. Is this what Gamma warned me about? I shook my head. "A what? I'm sorry, I don't have the slightest idea what you're talking about. Sounds too much like a fairy tale. And here I thought I was the only author in the room."

"Then this will still be fun if I'm wrong." Jax murmured before pulling my lips onto his.

The second our lips connected, a surge of the same electricity I sensed every time I touched him jolted through my body. I was never keen on dating, kissing more than my fair share of frogs in my lifetime really put a nail in the relationship coffin, but kissing Jax was indescribable. Of course, the rational me kicked in, managing to push Jax away while breaking our kiss. "Well, that was definitely something, but if you will excuse me, I need to go."

Jax sat back and laughed. "You are a very willful little thing, aren't you? Fine, you may leave and go wherever your heart desires, but don't get in my way when it comes to Julian. I can't protect you from him."

I raised my brow and tilted my head. "What do you mean when it comes to Julian? I thought you were his lackey?"

Jax let out a sigh. "I hate Julian. I'm deep under cover with his operation and I plan on bringing him down. I don't need you charging in here mucking things up. After I take care of him, I'll come for you, and we can pick back up where we left off before you so abruptly broke off our kiss. Father will be ecstatic when I tell him, besides handing him Julian, I will also be the one to break the curse."

The mention of the word curse gave me pause. Did Jax know about my supposed curse? "Wait, you're telling me you believe in curses? I thought you said you were a detective not a lunatic."

"Don't you? I mean, the curse is why you are here, isn't it? Your sister's case was just a convenient excuse to come seek me out. Why else would you come here and rent your sister's loft? It's not like you are an investigator, Tempest. I know you write crime dramas, but solving them is a whole different game. This is a dangerous situation. Julian isn't someone to trifle with."

I shrugged figuring my cover was pretty much blown. "I came here to bring Maria's killer to justice. I can't say I knew anything about a curse when I came."

Jax shook his head. "Well, it doesn't matter why you came here because together we are going to break the curse on both of our families."

Exasperated, I stood up from my place in the booth. "I have no intentions of doing anything about any curses, so please don't include me in your plans."

"Nice try, but we just forged a Fae pact here when you kissed me."

Folding my arms back across my chest, I tried to forget the amazing kiss and the way my heart fluttered. "Nice try, but I don't live in some mythical place called Fairy. I live in the land of the humans, right? So, no curse placed on me in Fairy could ever reach me here."

"Maybe you don't live in Fairy, but you don't have to live there to enact a Fae pact. You only need be in Fairy to seal a pact. And right now, you are standing in Fairy."

"What are you talking about? Aren't we still in your VIP room? You know the one inside your club in New York and not some place called Fairy."

"Yeah, we are in my VIP room, but this part is in a pocket dimension inside my territory in Fairy. I brought you here to test my theory. I could have played twenty questions, as you called it, at your apartment, but I needed you here to kiss you."

"You mean you brought me here with the sole desire to trick me into some kind of Fae pact?"

"Tempest, don't think of it as a trick. The magic wouldn't have worked if I kissed you outside of Fairy and the quickest way to get you into Fairy willingly was here at the club. You entered here of your own free will. I already told you I couldn't risk letting you get away before I could confirm my theory. At least not before I fully claimed you."

Throwing up my hands, I moved to the exit. "This is all ridiculous. Just stay away from me, Jax. I don't ever want to see you again." I heard Jax following me, though I didn't turn around.

"Tempest, please, wait."

When I reached the end of the hallway, Jax grabbed my arm and spun me around, forcing me to look up into his eyes. Their amber shade burned against the darkness. I didn't move to speak. I simply stared up at him.

"It's not safe for you to go on your own. You don't know how to get back to your loft. Let me take you back to the building. At least then I will know you're safe."

I shook my head. "What does it matter to you if I'm safe or not? You don't know me."

Jax ran his hands up my arms, causing my flesh to pimple before touching his head to mine. "I can't explain everything to you right now. I wish I could, but you won't understand half of what I tell you until we break the curse. But first, I must finish my mission in apprehending Julian. I can't have you snooping around like a bull in a china shop, especially not around somebody like Julian. You have no idea the horrors he is capable of."

"I think I do have some idea..." I noted sadly. "Maybe better than you."

Jax knitted his brows together. "What is that supposed to mean?"

I was tired and didn't want to argue anymore. I just wanted to go to sleep and leave this awful place. "Don't worry about it. Take me back to the loft. I'll leave first thing tomorrow as planned. I won't get in your way with Julian."

Chapter 14

Maria paced around the loft while I double checked I had everything I needed to leave.

"How could you give up so easily? So what if Jax knows who you are? He was bound to find out. You can't trust him to bring Julian to justice."

I paused, looking up at my sister. My eyes were puffy from crying all night, and it hurt to have them open. "Maria, just stop. I'm not equipped to solve your murder. I'm a crime novel writer. Ghosts tell me their stories and I write them down. Professionals, which clearly, I am not, do the actual crime solving. And if any of the stuff my Gamma told me about my bloodline is true, I can't afford to get sucked into Fairy. I need to leave here now and get as much distance as I can between Jax and myself. We'll just have to trust he's a man of his word."

Maria threw up her arms. If she had still been alive, the force of her movement would have caused her shoulders to crack. "You don't know him, Tempy! For all you know, he is just saying what you want to hear to get you to leave. Don't fall for his scare tactics."

Slamming my laptop closed, I threw it into my bag. "Maria, enough! I know what I promised you. Somehow, I will ensure Julian gets what he deserves, but I can't from here. I need to go back home, OK?"

Maria crossed her arms and shrugged. "Whatever, Sis. I'll see you after we get home."

Maria shimmered back inside the necklace, as I let out a sigh. I ran my fingers through my hair and pulled at a handful of the roots. The pain distracted me and helped clear my mind. I was glad I didn't have to wear the wig or contacts to fly home. My eyes hurt too much for the contacts anyway, so I opted to slide on my dark sunglasses. Hearing a ding, I looked down at my watch. I noted I had about thirty minutes to get to the airport. I pulled out my phone to check if my cab was on its way. I was so engrossed in the screen I didn't notice the body standing in my doorway until I walked straight into a well-defined chest. Dazed, I looked up to find a man who looked familiar, but who I couldn't place. He was tall with eyes the shade of amber, not unlike Jax, but this mystery man had blonde hair. "I'm sorry. I wasn't expecting anyone to be in my doorway. Please excuse me."

The man smiled before nodding his head. "It's alright, I can't say I blame you. I am not exactly an invited guest. My name is Julian and I own this building. I saw someone rented this loft and wanted to make sure you found everything satisfactory with the space."

Recognition dinged in my head. That's why he was familiar looking. This was Maria's Julian! I plastered on my best fake smile. "Yes, the space is lovely and while I would love to chat, I have a cab on its way to pick me up, so I hope you will pardon my abrupt departure."

Julian smiled before placing his hand on my shoulder. His touch sent shivers down my arm and not the good kind. His energy snaked down my arm like a slippery eel. I smiled again before moving to dislodge his hand. A message dinged on my phone. "Ah, see, my cab is here."

Julian squeezed my shoulder harder. "Your cab will wait. I want to talk to you."

My arm numbed, as if I had stuck it bare into a pile of snow. I raised my voice a little more than usual. "Hey, you're hurting me. How about you let go of me before I call the cops?"

Julian let out a laugh. "I own the cops in this sector, sweetheart. Don't worry, I'll make sure you get to where you need to be. I'll pay for the change in your plane ticket and the cab overages."

"That's very generous of you, but I really do need to be going. I have a family matter to attend to and I can't miss my flight. Maybe the next time I'm in town we can chat?" I turned to dislodge Julian's death grip on my shoulder, but nothing seemed to work.

"I have a better idea. Why don't we go to my office and talk like I asked? It won't take long, I promise. You can be back in Kentucky before tomorrow."

I arched my brow at Julian. "How do you know where I am going?"

"Did you believe the rental company would keep their end of the NDA," Julian smirked at me before leaning down close to my ear to whisper, "or that I wouldn't recognize my fiancée's stepsister?"

My breath caught in my throat at the mention of Maria. *Did Jax tell Julian about me*? "I don't know what you are talking about. I don't have any siblings. What did you say your name was? Julian?"

Julian smiled as he continued to drag me down the hallway. "I'd prefer not to discuss personal matters out here in the open. I promise to answer all your burning questions if you come to my office."

I didn't have much of a choice but to go along with Julian. I looked around, hoping someone would come out of their loft and at least distract this loser long enough so I could run. Unfortunately for me, it was a quiet time on the floor. I tried tapping into this mythical fae magic I owned by willing Julian to stop, but he just kept dragging me down the hallway. As we got closer to Jax's door, an idea struck me. Maybe if I accidentally ran my bag against the door, he would come out and rescue me. I hauled my bag up my arm the best I could and readied it to slip from my grasp. As soon as we were close to loft 34, I fake dropped my bag, smacking Jax's door with a resounding thud. Then, I quickly apologized as I tried to bend over and pick my bag up. "Oh, my goodness, I'm sorry, this bag is heavy, and I haven't gotten much sleep."

Julian sighed before bending over and picking up my bag. "Did you think you could run away if you dropped your bag, Miss Danvers?"

I shook my head, looking away from Julian's gaze while holding my breath, hoping Jax would open his door. When Jax's door didn't open, I let out a small sigh. Julian shouldered my bag and then tugged on my arm hard to get me to follow. "Ow! Stop hurting me, you jerk!"

"Keep your voice down, sweetheart, or you will disturb my friend and you don't want to meet him."

About the time Julian stopped talking, Jax opened the door. My heart jumped as I glanced up into his amber eyes. I wasn't very good at conveying emotion with my eyes, but I hoped I got my point across to him.

Jax raised a brow and looked from me to Julian. "Hey, Julian. I thought I heard your voice. Who's the chick? She your new girlfriend?"

Julian's shoulders relaxed as he turned to look at Jax. "No, you heartless bastard. She is a new tenant staying here for a short-term lease on Loft 36. I was just taking her to my office to discuss some business."

Jax nodded. He barely looked at me, and I saw no recognition in his eyes. He didn't even move to help me out of Julian's grip, which I thought was absurd, because I was pretty sure this is exactly what Jax warned me against. Gritting my teeth, I held out my hand towards Jax, plastering on a fake smile. "Hello, Jax. My name is Evelyn Potts. I was leaving to take care of some family business when I ran into

Mr. Devereaux here. Unfortunately, I don't really have the time in my schedule to talk to him, but he is insisting I go with him to his office."

Jax's brows knitted together, but other than the one gesture, his face remained emotionless. "I couldn't care less who you are or where you're going. If Mr. Deveraux wants to speak to you, though, I suggest you go to his office."

My fake smile faded from my lips as I let my hand fall. For some reason, Jax's aloofness hurt me more than I liked. I wasn't sure how to respond to him, but when Julian jerked hard on my arm, urging me to move, reality came back into focus. I grimaced as a tear slid down my face from the rough treatment. I took one last look at Jax before being dragged away and I could have sworn his amber eyes flashed red for a second. Julian continued pulling on my arm, which was now completely numb, directing me where to turn. Finally, after walking past the elevators and turning down several hallways, we reached a golden door. The plate attached had the name Julian Devereaux printed in a flowing script font.

Julian twisted the knob, allowing the oddly colored entry to swing open before shoving me inside. I looked around, finding myself standing in the middle of a royal blue office with plush carpet and golden accents. Looking up, I saw strange runes carved into the molding running along the ceiling. I bit on my lip to stop myself from crying. Is this what Maria felt before he killed her?

"You are a very interesting enigma, Miss Danvers. Whatever possessed you to give Jax an alias?"

"It's not an alias, Julian. I'm not sure who you think I am, but I assure you I'm not her."

My captor moved to sit at a dark mahogany desk in the middle of the room. It looked like something a president might sit behind. He leaned back in his chair before removing a cigarette from a golden box on the table. Snapping his fingers, the end of the cigarette lit.

"Miss Potts, as you called yourself, let's cut to the chase. I know who you are and why you are here. You are the stepsister to Maria Cardinal. Your name is Tempest Danvers, and you work as a best-selling author writing crime novels. You live in Kentucky in a small house on the property which your mother and stepfather own. And now you are temporarily renting the very loft where your sister died."

Sighing, I dropped my bag into one of the two empty chairs in front of the desk before depositing myself on the other chair. "Look, Julian, I think this is all a big misunderstanding. The rental agent told me someone died in the loft, but I assure you it wasn't anyone related to me. I came here for a brief vacation to see if I enjoyed living in this city. But honestly, I don't understand what appeals to anyone about New York. I find most things around here are loud, pushy, and overpriced. Now, if you will excuse me, I need to get back to tending to my business."

"Very well. I apologize for the confusion. However, if you walk out the door now, you'll never know why Maria Cardinal died."

The words stopped me in my tracks as a crushing pain stabbed into my chest. I was only seconds away from getting out of Julian's grasp and returning home. But, if I left now, I wouldn't find out why my sister died. I contemplated my choices, but Julian picked up on my hesitation.

"Tempest, stop thinking and sit back down. If you weren't Tempest Danvers, the mystery of Maria Cardinal and her death wouldn't pique your interest. I'm trying to help you here. I'd like to provide you with closure."

Turning, I ran my hands through my hair. Flopping back down on the chair, I glared at Julian. "Tell me how my sister died. And then tell me why you know so much about her death."

Julian smirked before taking a draw off his cigarette. Leaning forward, he blew the smoke at me across the desk. "I know because I killed her."

Chapter 15

The words, though I knew them to be true, tore through my heart. A sob escaped my mouth before I could choke it down. "Why would you kill her? I thought you loved her?"

Julian sat back in his chair, allowing his gaze to wander around the room. "I loved Maria enough for a human, but she stumbled on something she wasn't supposed to see. Unfortunately, what she saw couldn't be unseen and the laws of the land I am from dictated I had to kill her."

I crossed my arms over my chest hugging my sides trying to drive the chill Julian's words instilled in me. "Your explanation makes zero sense. For a human? Land where you're from? What are you like, an alien or something?"

"No, not quite. I'm from a land called Fairy and once upon a time I was a king. I held vast power in my hands until someone exiled me here to the land of humans. Because of my exile, I lost my connection with Fairy and most of my magical abilities. I've survived here by gathering the magic you humans call money. And now, I am once more a king of a vast empire."

I shrugged. "Still doesn't explain why you had to kill Maria. What did she witness that was so bad? I mean, she was going to marry you. Seems like she would have eventually found out all your dirty secrets and knowing her it wouldn't have phased her love."

Julian sat back and sighed. "I don't expect you to understand right now, but soon you will see everything with crystal clear eyes."

Shaking my head, I held up my hand. "Wow, you sound like a deluded old man. I have no idea why you thought any of this would bring me closure, but I'm done."

I stood up to walk out of Julian's office, regretting staying to hear his bullshit, but when I reached the door, I couldn't pull it open. I spun around, glaring at Julian, waiting for an explanation.

"I'm sorry, Tempest. I can't let you go. Not now that I am so close to being able to go back home."

"You don't need me to go back to Fairy or whatever you called it. It's not like I have a key to the place."

"Oh, but Tempest, that's where you are wrong. Finvarra, the King of the Summer Court, would grant any wish to the Fae who would bring him the key to ending the curse on his family. Which means you are my key back to Fairy."

"Sorry to burst your bubble, but I don't know where Fairy is. Now, open this door."

"I hardly believe you don't know anything about Fairy, but it would make more sense if you didn't. I knew the minute I saw you on a video chat with Maria you were different. Yet, it wasn't until I put my hands on you and felt a pulse of electricity for myself that I was sure of who you were. Of course, the background check Jax ran helped me confirm your identity when I saw the name of your grandmother."

I didn't want to waste another minute in this room with my sister's murderer, but I had no clue how to break out of the office. I was most definitely in over my head. Gritting my teeth, I ran towards the door and tried to throw my weight against it to force it open. When I bounced off, I could hear Julian laughing. Before I could turn around, he wrapped his hand around my arm. The cold, slinking feeling I experienced before returned, causing my body to shiver.

"Tempest, please, if you keep thrashing around like a wild beast, I will have to restrain you. I can't have you hurting yourself."

The longer Julian held onto me, the colder I became. Tears trickled down my cheeks, but I didn't know why. Spinning around, I looked up into Julian's eyes. "Let me go, you're hurting me."

Julian used his free hand to wipe the tears from my cheeks. "You are so warm, just like your sister. Did you know when a Fae loses their connection to Fairy, the loss fills them with nothing but coldness? This coldness makes it near impossible for us to touch another of our kind for very long. Before I met Maria, I was always cold. But you are as warm as autumn's second summer. Maybe I won't have to take you to Finvarra. Maybe I can keep you here. I wouldn't have to hide anything from you because you are Fae."

I pulled my arm, trying to remove myself from this nightmare. "I am not a Fae! Let me go!"

Julian leaned closer, burying his nose in my hair while simultaneously pulling on my arm to keep me still. My muscles tensed like a scared animal caught in a predator's gaze.

"I am sure I could change your mind in time. I can make you happy, Tempest. What happened with your sister was a tragedy. I didn't want to hurt Maria. Maybe I was rash to enforce the rules of Fairy when she found me smuggling illicit things in her dresses. It's not like Fairy could do anything more to me; I am already cursed and exiled. But maybe this was fate? Your coming here to learn more about her death has led you to my open arms. Perhaps this is the end of the curse for me? You are a lost daughter of the House of Autumn, and I was once a part of the Summer Court, after all."

The contents of my stomach churned, threatening to relocate to the front of Julian's shirt. The words of the curse my grandmother spoke of echoed in my mind. I took a deep breath, trying to gain control over my gag reflex. My entire body went numb from Julian's touch, and I didn't know if the coldness was from him or a natural avulsion to being wooed by my sister's killer. "You could never make me happy. Not after what you did to Maria. Whatever you have planned is simply folly."

Julian loosened his grip on my arm before wrapping both of his arms around my waist and pulling me against his chest. My face was now only inches from his as I stared up at him in horror.

"Shh. Don't look so shocked. I may not have all my powers, but I can make you forget Maria. A Fae never loses their innate abilities, and mine is memory alteration." Julian bent down, brushing his lips against mine.

As soon as his lips touched me, I jerked my leg up and into his manhood. Startled, Julian's grip loosened, and I used the event to move far away from him. I ran towards the window of the office, forcing the glass open. I had hoped to find a fire escape, but the only thing greeting me was a ledge and the open sky. Not wasting any time, I pulled myself up onto the windowsill, trying to reach the ledge. Maybe if I climbed to the next window, someone would let me into their loft. Of course, if I slipped, at least I wouldn't have to worry about trying to escape anymore. I had one foot on the ledge and was seconds away from hoisting myself out the window when the scent of an autumn breeze hit me. The smell caused me to lose momentum, which caused me to lose the grip I had on the trim of the window. I fell backwards as panic took over. The world spun around me until two hands grabbed onto my legs and pull me back through the window. After being dragged back inside, someone forced me to stand. I didn't want to look up because I was sure I would find myself in Julian's slimy grip, but a gentle hand pulled my chin up where I met amber eyes.

Warmth flooded my body helping me to relax my aching muscles. I blinked then squinted, not believing who held me. "Jax?"

Jax nodded before turning his gaze stone cold. "I caught her boss. She's unharmed."

"Thank you, Jax. Now, take her back to the lockup so she doesn't try any other daredevil tactics. I need to question her about her involvement in an apartment theft."

Jax turned and looked at Julian. "You think this little tartlet broke into someone's loft?"

"I have an eyewitness who described someone fitting her build breaking into your loft."

Jax turned his gaze back towards me. "Huh, must have been when I was out of town. I would have noticed a burglar this hot breaking in while I was home."

"You do seem to have an eye for the ladies, my friend. However, I would like to ask you to keep your paws off this one. Just place her in the holding cell while I decide what to do with her."

Jax's face remained emotionless as his gaze raked over me. "Yeah sure, boss. But if she stole anything from me, I might need some compensation."

"Give me a week or two to see what I can get out of her before you go making any plans for payments. She may just see the error of her way and return anything she took."

"Whatever, boss. Come on, trouble, you're going in the pokey." Jax said before dragging me towards a bookshelf.

I watched as Jax pulled a blue book, causing the shelf to slide to the right, to reveal a hidden opening before he unceremoniously shoved me into the blackness. Once inside, a small blue light appeared, illuminating the room. The space was about the size of a walk-in closet and contained a small desk, a wooden chair, a nasty looking bucket, and a bed. Once I regained some of my sense, I charged towards where Jax still stood watching me. I made it all the way over to him before I ran into his hands.

"You sure are a feisty one, aren't you? Don't worry, you'll be safe in here. Use this time to figure out whether you want to comply with Julian and where you stashed anything you took from my loft."

My mouth fell open in disbelief. Was Jax going to leave me here? I slammed my fists into Jax's chest, yelling at him. "You can't put me in here. You don't have the right!"

Jax smirked before pulling up his shirt and flashing me a badge attached to his belt. "I have every right to place you in a holding cell while you are being investigated. I am a police officer and I work security for Julian. Oh, just so you know, you can scream all you want, but the room is soundproof. Your sister learned about it the hard way. Shame, she always had such a pleasant voice."

Jax shoved me hard, knocking me off my feet, causing me to fall backwards. I caught myself on the bed, but my head still hit the wall. A deep thud followed by a sharp pain caused me to let out a wail. I reached my hand up to the back of my head. When I pulled my fingers back, I felt something sticky covering them. One look at the blood and I passed out on the bed.

Chapter 16

"Tempest, wake up! This is no time to be sleeping."

I rolled over onto my side, pulling a pillow over my face. "Come on, Maria, give me like five more minutes. My head is killing me."

"Tempest Danvers, if you don't get up right now, I will haunt you for the rest of your days. And from what Gamma Tempest told me, you might live an eternal life."

The words Gamma Tempest and haunt rolled around in my head as I tried to figure out why Maria would know anything about my grandmother or why Maria would threaten to haunt me. She didn't know I talked to ghosts and she sure as heck had never spoken to my grandmother. I tried to stretch, but when I accidentally bumped the side of my head, a sharp pain shot through me. I wondered why my head hurt so much, but then a flurry of events ran through my mind. Jolting up, I looked around to find myself not in my bed, but in a tiny room. Turning my hand over, I found the blood had dried and was now caked on my skin. "Maria?"

A shadow moved in the corner. "I'm here, Tempy. How's your head?"

"Like a semi ran over my skull. What the hell, Maria. This isn't what I signed up for."

"I know, Sis. I'm sorry. If I had known you were Fae, I would have never asked you to come here."

"Wait, do you know about the Fae?"

"A little, but I didn't know a lot until after I spoke to your grandmother."

I rolled my head around, trying to alleviate some of the stiffness. "Where did you learn about Fae before Gamma talked to you?"

"From Jax."

My head snapped up at the name, but the pain caused me to groan and grab my head. "You knew Jax?!"

Maria nodded before coming to hover next to me. "When I was still alive, I asked Jax to help me. I didn't know he was working for Julian when I approached him. Jax even tried to steer me away from digging into Julian's affairs, and for a while, I stopped looking. Yet, I still ended up here in this same little detention cube. I'm pretty sure Jax ratted me out to Julian. I remember arguing with Julian and then being shoved in this room. I don't understand why I have so many weird memories. Tempy, I think I died in this room."

"Julian told me he can change people's memories. Maybe he messed with yours and now you remember both your real and your false memories. Might be why your timeline never added up with what we knew about your death. But I don't guess any of that matters now. I thought Jax was someone I could trust, but I guess I was wrong. I should have listened to Gamma."

Maria nodded. "Memory manipulation would make sense. Look, Tempy, I'm sorry I drug you into this. Mom will never be able to get over losing you."

I shook off the pain and stood surveying the room. "I'm not dead yet, Sis."

A flash of bright white light appeared in the corner. The light formed into the shape of a woman before a voice came out of the light. "You sure as hell aren't dead yet, Tempy. Let's keep it this way."

The powerful light made me squint my eyes, but I knew the voice. "Gamma Tempest?"

"Oh Tempy, this is exactly why I didn't want you to have anything to do with Jax. We need to get you out of here before they pull you into Fairy."

"I'm sorry, Gamma. I thought I could trust Jax. Julian was ranting and raving about me being the key to his return to Fairy. All I was trying to do was leave."

Maria sighed. "I bet they sent Jax to find out if you were Fae and then he reported back to Julian with his findings. Why else would Julian show up the minute you were trying to leave? He never took that much interest in anyone's schedule, not even me."

Gamma shook her head. "No use crying over spilled milk now. We need to find a way for Tempest to break out of this room. Maria, do you remember anything about your time here?"

"No, not really. I only recall bits and pieces. I remember being in the dark and afraid."

As I crossed my arms, I sighed. "Well, we can check those off the list because we are in the dark and I am definitely afraid."

"Tempy, have you had any luck trying to use magic to leave this room?"

I raised a brow. "Gamma, I haven't had time to figure anything out about magic."

"Are you sure you didn't tap into any of your magic?"

I gritted my teeth as the pounding pain in my head started up again. Sadness washed over me. "No, all I did was meet with Jax at his nightclub. He wanted me to stay away from Julian. I came back home, and I got up today hoping to leave this place."

Gamma sighed. "Are you sure he didn't take you to Fairy?"

Pain radiated through my head as I tried hard to remember what exactly happened with Jax. "I must have hit my head hard, because I can't remember much about what happened. I remember him getting very close to me and then nothing."

"Damned Jax. He must have done something to your memory. Regardless, Tempy, I believe Jax took you inside Fairy somehow."

Aching, I stood up, pacing in a circle. I felt like the room was closing in on me. "What gives you that idea, Gamma?"

"Your aura has changed since the last time I saw you. It glows with a tiny, golden spec in the middle. Only Fae from Fairy have golden specs in their auras."

"If I went to Fairy, then why am I not still in Fairy at some Summer Court? Didn't you say if I ever went to Fairy, they would pull me into the politics of the realm?"

Gamma stammered. "I, I don't know. The curse said any Lost Daughter of House Autumn crossing over into Fairy would remain a part of Fairy forever."

"Which doesn't sound like a trap to me, but what do I know? I'm a dead human!" Maria snarked.

I paced back and forth, trying to remember anything about the night with Jax. I came up with nothing useful, but then the conversation with Julian niggled at the back of my mind. "What if the curse has something to do with my supposed Fae magic? Julian said when he lost his link to Fairy, he lost most of his magic, except for what he called his innate abilities. Maybe if I somehow entered Fairy, it's not that Fairy would pull me in, but maybe I'd gain a connection to the place? For a moment, Julian was adamant about taking me to Fairy and breaking some curse. Gamma, what exactly can you tell me about the curse? Don't leave out any of the details."

"Kinara, a daughter of House Autumn, was pledged to marry Oberon. Oberon was King of the Summer Court. However, she loved a mortal she had met in the land of humans. Kinara shirked her royal duties and ran away from Fairy. She glamoured herself to keep her identity hidden. King Oberon felt slighted and when Kinara did not return to him, he chased after her, but her glamour kept him from finding her. By the time Oberon found Kinara, she was already pregnant with a child from her human lover. Enraged, Oberon cursed every daughter in the House of Autumn from her lineage to fall inexplicably in love with the royals of the Summer Court for all of eternity if they ever stepped foot back inside Fairy."

I chewed on my bottom lip while processing the information from the curse, along with the information I learned from Julian. An idea flashed through my mind. I wasn't sure it was correct, but it felt right. "If what Julian said was true about his magic and the connection to Fairy, then these cursed daughters of House Autumn would have to choose between their powers or living here in the mortal world. Which if I went into Fairy, I could explain the new aura change. What it doesn't explain is why I'm not head over heels in love now."

"Hey, Sis. I know you want to solve this riddle and all, but as I see the situation, the conundrum can wait until after we get you out of here. If you have magic now, I'd suggest trying to use your powers. Worry about staying alive and not whether you are going to fall in love with some random prince. Maybe Gamma Tempest can use her magic to guide you out of here?"

Her words of wisdom made sense. None of this would matter if Julian or Jax came here to kill me. I needed to get out of here. "You're right. Is there anything you can help me learn, Gamma?"

"My powers are limited, but I could use an echo-bounce spell to help you see hidden items."

I took in a deep breath. "There has to be a hidden button or something in here. I mean, it must open in case you accidentally trap yourself in here."

"Unless it only opens with magic!"

I scowled. "You're not helping, Maria!"

Maria threw up her hands in defense. "Sorry, I'll be in my necklace."

Gamma held out her hands pulling my attention back to her. "Alright Tempy, close your eyes and reach out with your mind. Try to find anything my spell has lit up for you."

Closing my eyes, I tried to center myself and will whatever abilities I had to help me out of this predicament. After a few seconds, an odd warm sensation crawled up my spine, running throughout the rest of my body. When I opened my eyes, I found the once dark room bathed in a golden shimmer.

"Do not be alarmed," Gamma Tempest whispered. "I suspected this might happen. Your magic is reacting with the spell I placed and lighting up the room for you. You need to look for anything which isn't covered in your golden magic, as this means you've found magic cast by another user."

Scouring the room, I checked every nook and cranny, but didn't find anything outside of the golden shimmer. "I am not seeing anything in here outside of this golden glow. I don't see anything I can use to pry the door open. This is hopeless. Maybe I can rush them when they open the door. I don't think they would expect me to try brute force again."

"Do not give into despair, child. Despair is the killer of all magic."

"Yeah, but I'm all out of ideas and apparently my magic is no good. What else can I do, Gamma?"

Gamma Tempest didn't have time to respond before the mechanism on the door started turning. Hearing my cue, I stood up and readied myself to rush out the door. There was no way I was dying in this cell. Adjusting myself so I would not run into Jax or Julian's chest, I pumped my legs and ran straight towards my one chance. Something pulsed through my muscles, but I didn't have time to wonder if the sensation was my magic coming to life. My entire focus was on getting out of this room and never looking back. The door swung fully open as I made my dash towards the left side of the opening. I didn't look up to see who was at the door before squeezing past them and out into Julian's office. I heard someone calling my name, but I couldn't turn back at that point. Lucky for me, the door to the hallway stood open. As I careened down the hall, I didn't let up on my pace. I had no intention of taking the elevator, but I remembered a stairwell door on my way to the office earlier. When I saw the emergency sign, I smiled and charged towards the door. Once at the door, I slammed it open, causing a cacophony of sirens and alarms to trigger. Chaos was just what I needed to escape this horrid place, sight unseen.

Chapter 17

Cool air breezed across my face as I finally made it down the six flights of stairs and out the back door. The sun had already set, causing a slight chill. I no longer had my coat or my bag, but I kept moving. The stitch in my side demanded rest, but I refused to slow down until I was far enough away from Julian and Jax. A sizeable crowd of angry looking rich folks stood on the sidewalk all in different states of dress. Maurice barked orders to residents while sirens wailed. I moved in the opposite direction of the mob, slowing my full-on panic run to a medium walk. Directionless, I became hell bent on moving forward. I almost didn't notice when Maria appeared next to me.

"Wow, Sis, I didn't think you were a track star. Busting out of a room and running down six flights of stairs. I'd be on the ground dying right now if I weren't already dead. How are you still moving?"

I shook my head, hoping I wouldn't look like a crazy person on the street when I started talking to myself. "I don't know. Something surged through my body and kept me moving. My side is killing me, though. Is there anywhere I can get some water around here?"

"If you keep heading this way, you can go into Penn Station. You will blend in there and nobody will question your shabby appearance. You can grab some food and come up with a plan to get out of here."

I dug around in my pockets, searching for any of my possessions. Relief washed over me when my hand landed on the edge of my phone. I pulled out the case to find the wallet intact with my ID, credit card, and some cash. My phone, however, was deader than a doorknob. "At least I have my ID and some funds. Hopefully, I can book some kind of transportation out of here tonight."

"It's still fairly early in the evening for this place. Your best bet is probably to find something to eat and then take a train ride out of here to somewhere else. You can go directly back to Kentucky."

I turned when I saw the sign pointing to the entrance of the travel station. The hustle and bustle of the place allowed me to relax, and I sighed in relief. I turned to find Maria no longer by my side, but I didn't worry. There were maps all over the place and at this point, I was sure I could find my way around. Of course, I didn't need them because I was apparently close to both the train customer service and several food places. The thought of food had my mouth watering. I didn't know what day it was or how long it had been since I had eaten. I moved towards a heavenly smell but stopped for a second when I realized there was a police station inside the terminal. A lump formed in my throat at the thought of Jax sending out his buddies to look for me.

Trying to look less like a criminal and more like a tourist, I spun around until I eyed a bookstore selling various sundries. I grabbed a touristy t-shirt, a cord for my phone, a small pre-charged battery pack, a brush, a pack of wet-wipes, and a bottle of water. I just needed to get this stuff and run into the nearest bathroom to clean up. Then I would figure out what smelled so delicious out there and buy some of whatever it was to sate my now grumbling tummy. I flopped all my stuff onto the counter and tried to act natural.

The girl at the cash register smiled at me as she started ringing up my purchases. "You have a most interesting array of goods here, lady. Lemme guess, they lost your baggage from the train?"

I frowned at the girl. I didn't want to make small talk. I wanted to blend into a crowd. "Yeah, no, I lost my bag myself on my trip here, but it's OK. I just need a few things to get me through until my train leaves and I can go back home."

The cashier took her sweet time scanning my items and shoving them into a cloth bag. She pushed the bag towards me before telling me the total. I swiped my card, counting down the seconds, willing the transaction to go faster. Finally, the card reader beeped a loud noise. I reached for my bag, but the girl frowned as she grabbed the bag back towards her.

"They declined your card. Do you have another card you could try?"

Huffing, my shoulders slumped. "Does it say why?"

"No, it just says declined. I'm sorry, but unless you have some other way to pay, I have to void this out."

Crap, without my credit card, I wouldn't be able to book a ticket home on anything. I cursed under my breath as I dug around for the cash I had in my wallet. Pulling out a fifty-dollar bill, I sighed as I handed it over to the girl. I would have to charge my phone and log into my account to find the problem with my card. The girl handed me back my two dollars in change and that's when my stomach made itself known. Heat flushed through my cheeks.

"I'm sorry. I haven't eaten for a few hours. Whatever food I keep smelling is not helping matters, either."

The girl nodded with almost pity in her eyes. "It's probably the pizza place down the way. They have the most amazing pizza. Unfortunately, you won't be able to get much there with two dollars."

I'm sure by this time the girl thought I was some kind of scroungy beggar. I could feel my hair was a mess, and I wondered if I had blood on my shirt from the scuffle between me and Jax. She might think, since the cards wouldn't work, I stole the phone and try to call the police. I flashed my biggest smile and shook my head at the cashier. "I have plenty of money and once I get my phone charged, I can fix the credit card issue with my bank. They might have blocked the sale because I didn't notify them I had to work in New York this week."

The girl flashed me a rather uneasy smile. "Yeah, maybe. Good luck to you. I hope you get your card fixed."

The hairs on the back of my neck stood up as the girl flashed her smile at me. Something was wrong, but I didn't know what. I grabbed the bag, nodded, and took off towards the bathroom I passed on my way into the terminal. Unfortunately for me, the bathroom was on the other side of the police station. I tried to nonchalantly pass without looking towards the station, but when someone called out my name, I looked up in a knee-jerk reaction. My heart sank as I found the person yelling my name was none other than Jax. Why did there have to be a police station in here? I shook my head and kept walking towards the restroom, but Jax moved to grab my arm.

"Tempest, stop running away from me. I'm not here to hurt you."

Those words broke something inside me, remembering how he treated me so indifferently before. "Really, Jax? Because I have a gash in the back of my head that says otherwise. Now, let me go so I can go clean up and buy a ticket out of this hellhole."

Jax didn't let go of my arm. "Tempest, please, they have alerted Julian about you being here. You need to come with me. I have a plan."

"Yeah, I figured that's why you're here, because you're Julian's goon, remember? Neither of you can cause a scene out here in this very public spot; so, I suggest you let me go and we count our losses. You can tell Julian you didn't get here in time, and I left for an unknown location. It's the least you can do since I know you betrayed Maria. Or does the thought of another dead woman not bother you?"

"I didn't betray your sister. I tried to help her out of a dangerous situation, same as I am doing for you. Only you won't end up dead at the hands of Julian. You'll just end up his captive forever."

I jerked my arm hard to pull out of Jax's grasp. "And, what, him keeping me hostage bothers you? Sure didn't seem like it when you locked me in his torture chamber."

"I don't have time for this, Tempest. We have to go now before Julian's other guys get here. I will explain everything to you if you just please come with me. I've booked you a room a few minutes from here. You'll be safe there because Julian can't enter the facility."

I wanted to hate Jax and not believe a word he said, but something in my gut told me I should go with him. At least a hotel where Julian couldn't enter would have a shower and food. I'd probably be better able to schedule a flight out of this crazy place if I had access to a hotel with a phone. "Fine, I'll go with you, but no funny business. If you double cross me again, it won't be pretty."

Jax nodded before waving his hand over my head. "Come on, follow me."

"What did you just do?"

"I glamoured you to look like one of Julian's female associates. It'll be less suspicious if people notice me leaving with a known colleague rather than the woman he has everyone out looking for."

I let out a grunt. "Making me look like a hooker is better?"

"Michelle is not a hooker. She's a companion. And nobody will question me about leaving with Michelle and going to a hotel Julian can't enter."

I raised my brow. "And why wouldn't it be odd exactly? If she's Julian's err companion, shouldn't she *not* go to a place he can't get into?"

Jax shrugged. "She took up residence at the St. Mary's Highrise awhile back when she learned Julian couldn't get in there. She was mad at him and wanted to teach him a lesson. Unfortunately for her, the stunt didn't bother Julian one bit."

"Julian doesn't seem the type to let something like that go. How did she get away with it?"

Not missing a beat, Jax kept walking towards the hotel. He sighed for a moment before running his hand through his hair. "He stopped caring about his companions once he proposed to Maria. Which made Michelle upset because she thought she should be the one marrying Julian. So, she did the one thing she knew would make Julian mad. Only the stunt backfired, and Michelle is too stubborn to move out of the place now. She likes to take anyone in Julian's employ back to her suite, so Julian is sure to hear about her antics. Michelle believes at some point her little game will cause Julian to change his mind and take her back."

I nodded, not knowing what to say. In less than five minutes, we had arrived at St. Mary's. The building had a modern look for such an odd name. "Why can't Julian get into this place?"

"Associates of the Summer Court run the building and they despise Julian. They warded the whole place to keep him specifically off the grounds. Julian can't even walk down this part of the sidewalk."

"Why would the Fae have a hotel in the human world?"

Jax shook his head. "Not Fae, associates of the Summer Court."

I shrugged. "What's the difference?"

"The Pixie Alliance runs this place, and they hate Julian because he steals Pixies and sells them as food to other exiled supernaturals." Now come on, let's get inside and up to the room before anyone sees through your glamour.

Jax's words swirled around in my mind. *Pixies hate Julian because he sells them as food for other exiled creatures.* I couldn't imagine how awful it would be to be sold as food. Lost in thought, I chewed on my nails on the elevator ride up to the top floor of the hotel. I didn't hear the elevator ding until Jax pulled on my arm to get my attention.

"Come on, this is our stop."

Jax unlocked the door with his keycard. I followed behind him, still thinking about the Pixies. My brain finally put two and two together a moment later. "Pixies. That's what Julian was smuggling in Maria's dresses?"

Jax nodded as he collapsed onto a nearby couch. "Go get cleaned up. I brought your stuff here so you could change. I'll work on fixing your bank cards."

"Wait, what? You did something to make the store reject my credit card? How?"

Jax looked up with a grin on his face. "I'm a cop, Tempest. We have our resources. I put the block on your card so I could find you quicker. I figured you'd be trying to hightail it out of here, and the closest place to do that would be Penn Station."

I shook my head before turning around to make my way into the bathroom to grab a much needed shower. I gritted my teeth and mumbled as I walked away. It shouldn't surprise me Jax was involved in foiling my escape. As I closed the bathroom door, I heard a laugh from Jax. I was glad my predicament amused him so, but I wondered if he would laugh after I had him thrown in jail for the murder of my sister.

Chapter 18

I stood under the showerhead until my skin felt like it was on fire. After a few more minutes, I turned off the water and stepped out to wrap myself in a large fluffy robe. I would have to look into getting one of these high-pressure rain shower heads at home. The thought of home made me sigh. I grasped the necklace still around my neck. "I'm in way over my head, Maria. What am I even doing here?"

Maria appeared sitting on the marble vanity. "I'm sorry, Tempy. I shouldn't have insisted you come here. This whole thing is a colossal mess, and somehow, I feel it might be my fault. If I hadn't met Julian, none of this would be happening now."

I threw my head back. "Maria, this isn't your fault. I thought I could come up here and solve a mystery. Neither you nor I knew about my grandmother's secret or some crazy family curse. Honestly, I just want to get home and put this behind me. I don't want to think about Fairy, Fae, Pixies, or New York ever again."

Maria jumped down from the counter. "I know all of this is crazy. At least you have another book you can write."

I laughed at the suggestion. "I'm not so sure a book filled with crazy Fae and family curses would sell to my current audience. I'd almost have to launch a new pen name with a supernatural spin."

"I bet if you pitched this story to your publisher, they'd chomp at the chance to publish it. It's almost so wild they just might believe the story."

I dug around in my bag, pulling out a clean t-shirt and a pair of my favorite cargo pants. "Let's focus on getting out of this place alive first. I wish you could book me a flight out of here. Walking through walls is super helpful for spying, but not so much for actual escaping and travel booking."

"Hector told me there are some ghosts who can touch things, but they are usually pretty crazy. They use part of their remaining life force to interact with items, but eventually it dissolves their essence."

I frowned. "I definitely wouldn't want you to dissolve."

Maria looked down at her feet. "What exactly do you want me to do once you get back home?"

I tugged on my shirt before turning around and giving Maria a questioning look. "What do you mean?"

"I don't know. You can't be talking to your dead sister forever, you know?"

I rubbed my forehead. "We'll cross that bridge when we get there. Right now, I'm not out of the woods, or maybe I should say Fairy. Let's focus on getting me back home and away from this circus. Now, back in the necklace with you until I know it's safe again."

I paused at the door to collect myself before walking back into the room where I left Jax. Only he was no longer sitting on the couch. I looked around, but I didn't see him anywhere in the room. I smirked, thinking this was a test to see if I would escape, and the minute I went for the door, Jax would pop out and capture me again. My stomach rumbled in protest while I debated my choices. Sighing, I gave up and picked up the menu for room service. If I was going to have to stay here, I would get a good meal. I perused the menu, finally deciding on a steak with shrimp. Picking up the phone, I dialed the front desk.

After two rings, a voice came through. "Front desk. How may I help you?"

"Yes, I'd like to order a well-done steak with a side of shrimp to be sent to my room." I prayed they knew what room I was calling from because I had no clue.

The voice on the other end replied. "And what room are you staying in, please?"

Damn. Would I sound like a crazy person if I didn't know? "Uhm, well. Hold on a moment."

I heard a sigh come from the other end of the line when I set the receiver down to find the number of the room on the front of the door. I had almost made it to the door when a breeze blew through the room, followed by the potent scent of cool autumn wind. Turning around, I found Jax picking up the phone.

"My apologies. My wife didn't know the number. She's jet lagged. We are in suite 700. Send up two of whatever she ordered, along with a bottle of Chateau Blanc." Jax hung up the phone before looking up at me.

I stood there with my arms crossed and a brow raised. "Your wife?"

"Makes it more plausible to have a married couple in this suite and less likely for Julian's cronies to figure out we're here. Don't worry, I'm glamoured. Nobody will know it's me."

"If you're glamoured, why do you still look the same to me?"

Jax paused and frowned. "You can't see my glamour? Interesting."

"Why is that so interesting?"

"Only those with high-level veil piercing magic can usually see through a glamour, and there are only a handful of Fae in all the courts with the ability to see beyond. I wouldn't expect a mixed bloodline Fae, even one from the House of Autumn, to have enough power for that kind of ability."

I shrugged. "I don't understand anything you just rambled on about. Maybe it's just a fluke."

Jax shook his head while mumbling to himself. He squinted his eyes while staring a hole through my soul. "Unbelievable. That makes sense, though."

I rubbed the goose pimples from my arms. "I'm sorry. What makes sense? I'm confused. And can you stop boring a hole through my very core while you're at it?"

Jax's gaze flew up to my eyes, searching for something. "You felt me looking at you? Nobody should be able to detect when I use my Eye of Examination."

I stood there under Jax's wandering gaze, feeling exposed though I had on all my clothes. He moved closer to me. When I tried to shrink back, he grabbed my arm, holding me in place. Unlike before, when his touch electrified me, heat now ran through my body and pooled in places I wasn't expecting. The smell of leaves in the fall invaded my nose as I stood locked in this weird stance with Jax. His free hand moved up to caress my left cheek, causing more heat to fill my body. I had no clue what was going on, but Jax wasn't backing up and neither was I. I stood rooted in place as Jax brought his lips closer to mine. My breath hitched in my throat when our lips touched. I reached out, fisting his shirt when the need to have him closer washed over me. Accepting the invitation I apparently provided, Jax wrapped his arms around me before lifting me up and carrying me over towards the couch. He sat down without breaking our kiss. The next thing I knew, I was straddling him, desperately trying to unbutton his shirt. I almost had all of Jax's buttons undone before a loud voice startled me.

"Tempest Danvers, I told you not to get involved with Jax!"

Shock ran through my body as I snapped out of whatever trance I had been in. "Gamma? What are you doing here?"

"Stopping you from making a mistake, Tempy. You do not want to entangle yourself with him. You give into him now and you are stuck with him forever. Fae mate for life under our laws."

I pushed myself away from Jax and stood up to walk towards my Gamma, not worrying about Jax seeing me talk to my dead grandmother. "What are you talking about? I'm not mating with anyone."

"Child, what do you think you were about to do? Didn't your mother teach you anything about sex?"

I threw up my hands. "Woah! I wasn't going to sleep with him."

"You weren't?" I heard Jax ask from the sofa.

I spun around to face Jax only to find him leaning back on the sofa, his shirt fully open, with an incredulous look on his face. "You're more worried about me saying I wasn't going to sleep with you than seeing me talk to thin air?"

Jax rolled his eyes before scrubbing his hand over his face. "Tempy, I know you talk to ghosts, and I'm guessing your beautiful grandmother Tempest is chastising you for getting close to me. I'm not surprised. She never did like me much."

"Time out here, gang. How do you know I can talk to ghosts, Jax? And what do you mean my grandmother doesn't like you? You're like in your twenties and she died over twenty years ago. You would have been a kid when she died."

Jax rubbed his hands through his hair. "You were telling the truth when you said you didn't know anything about Fairy. Look, I know you can talk to ghosts because I put two and two together when you said you could see through my glamour. Only those with veil piercing can see through glamour. That's a rare gift in and of itself, but communication with the dead is the rarest and most sought-after gift in all of Fairy. The fact this seems to be your innate magic is incredible. When I take you back to Fairy, I can only imagine how much power you will have. You may be more powerful than the legendary Titania herself."

"Uhm. Cool. I think. But what makes you think I'm going back to Fairy with you?"

"Because of our Fae pact made at my club, remember? I claimed you as mine and you agreed to come with me back to Fairy. How else am I supposed to break the curse on the Summer Court? One of the princes of Summer must marry a Lost Daughter of Autumn and help her accept her powers. Tempest, if you accept your full magic, you can break the curse on both of our families. But only if you come back to Fairy and marry me."

"First, I don't remember making any kind of agreement with you. I remember you taking me to your club and kissing me. Then I remember being mad at you and getting ready to go home, only to be kidnapped by Julian. Come to think of it, Julian said some crazy things about taking me back to Fairy because I was the key home for him. I have news for the both of you. I'm not going to Fairy and I'm not marrying either of you."

Jax tilted his head and scowled. "What do you mean, marry Julian? Did he tell you he intended to marry you?"

I let out a sigh before moving over to one of the wingback chairs and sitting down. "Julian said a lot of messed up things, including him wanting to keep me here with him. He told me he could make me happy and that he could make me forget Maria."

"What a jackass! I've only been dead for a year." Maria appeared next to me. If I didn't know any better, I'd think she was putting off heat with the face she was making.

"Maria, stop. You are giving me a headache." A wave of nausea washed over me like a tidal wave, forcing me to put my head between my knees. I hadn't had a panic attack in years, but all this talk about mates, curses, and magic was taking a toll on me. A knock at the door brought me out of my spiral.

Jax got up and walked over to the door to accept the room service. The aroma of steak filled my nose, causing my stomach to once again pipe up. Despite my panic attack, my body demanded food.

Jax wheeled the tray over to the small dining table by the balcony. I watched as he placed the plates down and pulled out a chair for himself. "Tempest, eat. You didn't eat at the club the other night and you spent a whole day in the holding cell. I know you must be starving. Come over here and sit down, please."

I looked up at Jax and then at my Gamma. I sat there frozen, unable to process the information and unable to will myself to move.

"Tempy, please go eat something. You are exhausted and not able to think clearly at this point. You need to eat and rest before you try to understand everything you just learned. I'll leave you two alone so you can have some peace. I'm so sorry, Tempy, I thought keeping you in the dark about everything would keep you safe. I never thought the curse would come knocking on your door, literally."

As I looked at my grandmother, I tried to hold the tears back. "And yet here we are."

Chapter 19

After I ate, I excused myself to step out onto the balcony. The cool breeze helped numb the pain in my body. I could feel autumn coming in the air. I always loved the season and now, knowing what I did about The House of Autumn, my love of the season made sense. Part of me buzzed with excitement over the thought of me having magic, but there was another part of me who wished I'd never come here. My life was so simple a few weeks ago. My biggest concern was what story I would write next. But now? Everything was so messed up. I didn't want to hate Jax, but I wasn't sure I wanted to marry him for the greater good, either. So, I decided for now I was just going to stand on the balcony and enjoy my view of the city that never sleeps. Something warm wrapped around me, bringing me out of my thoughts. I realized Jax had wrapped a blanket around my shoulders.

"I didn't want you to get too cold out here. Fae Flu is no fun."

I kept my face trained towards the skyline as I responded. "Thank you, but don't worry, I've never been one for catching any kind of flu."

I heard Jax turn to walk back inside, but then he paused and took in a deep breath. "Tempest, I'm sorry. I thought you knew about the curse when I made the pact with you. I figured you came here to New York looking for me. After you broke into my loft and opened the charmed box, I was sure the curse was leading you. It didn't occur to me you might have come because a ghost led you here."

"Why did you bring me Maria's necklace?"

"I got to know Maria pretty well during her time here and she told me the story behind the necklaces. You meant a lot to her, and I thought it would bring you some comfort to have the pendant back."

I spun around to glare at Jax. "I mourned her for an entire year and was finally making something of my life again. And then you showed up with that damned necklace. Why did it take you a year? Why not give it to me when we came up here to claim her body?"

"I didn't want Julian to know I had the necklace. It would have been an unpleasant situation if he knew I still had Maria's pendant."

"Because he ordered you to burn the necklace, right?"

Jax nodded. "Julian knew how much Maria loved the necklace, and he suspected you might be a Fae. He didn't want to risk Maria attaching herself to the pendant and spilling her secrets to you. Julian thought maybe you knew about Fairy and would somehow turn him over to the Fae Courts."

I paced back and forth, chewing on my nails. "Was Julian mad when he found out you gave me the necklace?"

"Not really. The minute he found out you arrived here in town, he became focused on meeting you and luring you into his elaborate scheme to get back into Fairy. That's why I took you to my club. I wanted to get to you before he could. I was hoping to move you out of town before he tried to make his play for you. But that damned Johnny ratted you out to Julian. He saw you breaking into my apartment, and he saw you leave with me. Julian trusts me, but he didn't like the idea of me getting too close to you. He's a jealous guy."

"Who's Johnny? There wasn't anyone in the hallway when I broke into your loft. Well, outside of Maria and Hector."

"Johnny was Julian's business partner until he messed up and Julian killed him. Julian hired a necromancer to bind Johnny to do his bidding for all of eternity. Johnny is an enhanced specter and can hide from people like you. He wouldn't be any good to Julian if everyone with ghost talker abilities could see him."

"This Johnny must have been the one giving me a weird sense of being watched. I thought it was simply paranoia. I take it Julian knows I can talk to Maria."

"That's the one thing about Johnny; he can't see other ghosts and other ghosts can't see him. He lives in this weird limbo bound to Julian, and it somehow separates him from other ghosts. I don't think Julian wants his forced ghosts talking to other ghosts. Dark magic keeps the bound ghost in check, but there is no proof the ghost couldn't break away from their master if they got ideas and energy from other ghosts."

"OK, so what happens now? I'm guessing going home as long as Julian is looking for me isn't possible?"

"I had a plan, Tempest, but I don't think it will work now that I have a few more pieces of the puzzle. Plus, I don't want to force you into something you might regret. It was different when I thought you knew about the curse."

"So, your grand plan was to drag me back to Fairy, and then what?"

"I'd marry you, ending the curse on my family, and after you were safe inside Fairy, I'd be able to go back and capture Julian."

"Why would we need to get married? Why can't you take Julian back now and leave me here where I belong?"

"Because this damned curse colors my actions. I honestly thought I could have my cake and eat it, too. Believe me when I say I never set out to lure you here, but like Julian, I've always had my suspicions about you being Fae based on your pictures."

The longer Jax talked, the more my head pounded. I walked back inside to the mini-bar and swiped a cold soda from the selection. I didn't care if the drink cost Jax twelve dollars. After cracking open the lid, I took a long swig before turning around to face Jax again. "You brought me the necklace to see if I was a Lost Daughter, didn't you?"

"I didn't think it would hurt to check. If you were a Lost Daughter of House Autumn, it would be a win-win for me. Plus, I wanted to give you Maria's necklace again."

I sat my soda down and frowned before crossing my arms. "Did you kill Maria to get to me?"

Jax took a step back, throwing up his hands. "Woah, no, it wasn't like that Tempest. Julian killed Maria in his holding cell because Maria found some way to resist his memory wipe. Julian says he didn't want to break the rules of Fairy by letting a human know about his Fae business, but the truth is, Maria was very close to getting hard evidence, which would have allowed me to arrest Julian once and for all. I think he thought Maria was collecting the information somehow for you to use against him."

I scoffed. "I guess killing humans isn't against Fae law, then?"

"Not once a Fae invokes the rule of none shall know."

"How convenient for Julian in this situation. I guess he messed with Maria's memories enough to scramble her brain before he killed her so she couldn't tell on him. I still don't understand how you don't have enough evidence to arrest him. I mean, you're his cleaner, aren't you? Can't you testify against him?"

"Fae law forbids the arresting party to testify without corroborated evidence. I would need a witness statement or a rescued victim to testify as well. Once I have one of those two things, I can arrest him and force a trial to be held here since he can't enter Fairy. The problem is, Julian uses humans who don't know what they are seeing to do his dirty work. Maria was the only one to see him dragging a Pixie to slaughter. And well, the Pixies are usually dead before they're shipped out, so they can't testify."

"This is all ridiculous! This curse both keeps Julian out of Fairy and protects him from punishment while he wreaks havoc here in the human world, unchecked? Is everything so convoluted with the Fae?"

Jax's shoulder's slumped as he looked down to the floor. "I don't have a simple answer for you, Tempest. Navigating the politics of the Fae is tricky, especially for one who knows nothing of our laws."

Nervousness mixed with rage shot through my body. Throwing off the blanket, I paced around the hotel suite, grabbing at my hair. How could I be so close to bringing Maria's murderer to justice and yet failing at the same time? If only I could talk to a dead Pixie, or if Maria could remember all the details. Lack of sleep mixed with too much caffeine addled my brain a little, but at this point the idea I had couldn't be any kookier. "Gamma Tempest, I need you."

My grandmother's form flicked to life in front of me, her face still marred by regret. "Tempy, what can I help you with?"

"Is there any way I can make a spirit manifest for others to interact with them?"

Gamma Tempest's face fell. "Child, that path is full of the dark. You may possess the ability to talk to the dead, but I don't think you can control them long enough to have them take corporeal form. That's something only a channeler level necromancer can do after years of dark magic."

"Why is it dark magic? My magic isn't dark. If I could talk to ghosts without a connection to Fairy all this time, do you think if I obtained all my power, I could have a ghost give a statement so the Fae can deal with Julian?"

"If you went into Fairy and gained your magic, you could break the curse keeping Julian out of Fairy. Then Jax could testify against Julian in front of the Court because he would not be the arresting party. However, getting Julian into Fairy willingly to force a trial may pose a problem."

"I think I could lure him in there. Before he hatched the plan for me to stay here with him, he wanted to take me to King Finvarra to break a curse and gain a favor. I'm not sure how he would take me to the King if he couldn't get into Fairy, but I think Julian would come into Fairy if he thought he were going to be rewarded for his efforts."

Jax cleared his throat, causing me to look over at him. "Tempest, I don't like where your thoughts are going. I can only hear one part of the conversation, but making a deal with a Fae like Julian, even if he is a cursed exile, is dangerous."

"Tempy, listen to Jax. He's right on this account. You can't outsmart Julian to trick him. You'll end up in more trouble."

"Not if I go into Fairy and accept all my magic. Everyone keeps telling me how powerful I am now, but I don't have most of my magic. Something deep down tells me the power I could wield is inside Fairy, waiting for me, but only if I ask for my birthright. I think Julian believes this as well. If I convince him to help me into Fairy with the promise of a reward for his deeds, I am sure he would come to me willingly."

Gamma Tempest scowled at me while shaking her head. "I dislike this plan, Tempest Danvers."

"Too bad. I'm tired of feeling like a pawn in everyone else's game. It's time for me to make a move. Jax, you're going to let Julian know you have me, and you are bringing me back. If he isn't interested in killing me at first sight, I should be able to convince him to help me get into Fairy. Once I'm inside Fairy, Jax can help me meet the courts and find my magic. Then I'll break the curse and invite Julian into Fairy where we can ambush him with the trial. Jax will testify and Julian will get what he deserves."

Jax shook his head. "If you are sure you want to do this, Tempest, I'll arrange for us to go back tomorrow."

With my mind made up, my nervous energy waned and the desire to sleep took root. "I'm sure. Make the arrangements. I'm going to get some sleep while I can."

Chapter 20

Nervous energy coursed through my core as I sat waiting for Julian to meet with me. I didn't like the idea of going back into Julian's office after the last time, but Jax promised me he wouldn't let Julian take me anywhere. I willed myself to sit still, despite wanting to chew through my nails. The sound of the doors opening made me jump.

"Miss Danvers, what a surprise to find you back in my office. I was sure after our last encounter I would never see you again." Julian winked at me as he sat down behind his huge wooden desk.

He got a weak smile from me. "I somehow doubt you were going to let me walk out of your life."

Leaning back in his chair, Julian grinned. "You are quite an interesting woman, Tempest. So, tell me what made you come back? Surely you haven't decided you'd like to be my mate?"

I couldn't stop the snarl forming on my lips. "No, I came here to ask you about Fairy. You said I could get you back into Fairy. I'm guessing from your ranting the other day about being a Lost Daughter from House Autumn you think I'm a Fae? What if I buy that story? What would me going to Fairy net me?"

Julian steepled his fingers while silently staring at me. "You really don't know, do you?"

I countered by clasping my hands onto my lap and looking into Julian's eyes. "I wouldn't be here asking you if I did, now, would I?"

"Your bloodline hails from Kinara, the treacherous Fae woman who caused this mess of a curse. Her actions bound me to the mortal plane and forced the women of your bloodline to live outside of Fairy."

"OK, that's interesting, but it still doesn't tell me what I could gain by going into Fairy. Or why you wanted me to go to Fairy so badly."

Letting out a sigh, Julian cast his gaze down to his desk, almost like he was trying to recollect an ancient memory. "Your bloodline bound me to this mortal plane exiling me from Fairy. If you go back into Fairy, the counter-curse I placed on your family will trigger and, eventually, I will return to Fairy."

Shifting in my chair, I leaned forward. "And what was this counter-curse?"

"All daughters from Kinara's line returning to Fairy are fated to fall inexplicably in love with princes from the Summer Court."

"So, I go back into Fairy, fall in love with a prince and what? You can waltz back in like nothing ever happened? Seems like I'm still getting the bum end of the deal here. I thought surely I'd get something other than a husband I don't want."

"You misunderstand me, Tempest. I believe once you go into Fairy, you will receive all your Fae magic. You don't have a connection to the land because you are cut off from Fairy. However, if you were to visit Fairy of your own free will, you would gain power. Then you could use this power to break the curse blocking me from entering my home."

I raised a brow. The information Julian gave me seemed to fit what everyone else had told me would happen. "Would this power be enough to protect those I love from harm?"

"I'll be honest with you, Tempest. I don't know how much power you would receive or how you would find your connection to the magic. But I truly believe there is power waiting for you inside Fairy and if you go there and claim it, I can finally be done with this curse."

"And if I claim my magic, would you leave me alone? Or would you pursue me for vengeance on my bloodline?"

Julian looked up at me with almost a wistful gleam in his eye before his voice softened. "I have no desire to quarrel with your bloodline any further. After Kinara's human lover died, I hoped she would come back to me. I didn't plan to spend three hundred years trapped in this mortal land. I'm ready to go home and I can only do that if you help me. Look, I can't go into Fairy with you, but I can send someone to help you find your way around."

"You have someone who can get into Fairy working for you?"

"Yes, in fact, you met him the other day when he caught you falling out of a window."

My face played dumb, but inside I smiled. Having Jax come with me knowingly could only be a boon to my plan. "Your goon Jax? He's a Fae?"

"Yes, he is one of the few Fae I employ. He's an excellent spy for me in both this realm and the Fae realm. The intel he can gather on the Courts is invaluable."

I tilted my head, trying not to frown. "Is he someone important?"

"Jax is the bastard son of the King of the Summer Court. He's the product of an illicit affair between the King of Summer and the Queen of Winter."

I tried to hide the gasp. I didn't expect Julian to know Jax was a Fae and from the Summer Court. "But if you send me in there to trek around with a royal from the Summer Court, does that mean I'm going to wind up married to him?"

"Oh, you sweet naïve girl, don't be silly. Jax isn't an actual prince from the Summer Court. He's a love child made from a hundred-year fling between two powerful people. That's why Jax works for me. He's an outcast in Fairy. Don't worry, the curse won't cause you to fall madly in love with him and if you play your cards right, you can avoid the Summer Court altogether."

I sat for a moment, processing all the information Julian provided to me. Gamma Tempest wasn't sure Julian would willingly go back into Fairy, but that's exactly what he wants. Jax warned me working with Julian would be tricky. I had to choose my next words carefully because I was about to make a deal with a devil. "Alright, let me get this straight. I go into Fairy and try to find my connection so I can claim magic you think is waiting for me. Then I can use said magic to break the curse blocking you from returning to Fairy. You will enter Fairy and collect everything you deserve but will leave me alone after I help you gain entrance into Fairy. And if all goes well, your counter curse will break, and I won't have to marry some random prince. Is this the deal?"

Julian stood up and extended his hand. "I, Julian Deveraux, promise to leave Tempest Danvers and her blood alone after she helps me re-enter Fairy."

I stood and eyed Julian's outstretched hand. The hairs on the back of my neck stood up. "Is there something you aren't telling me, Julian?"

"No, this is my oath to you, Tempest. Once we shake, an unbreakable contract will form between us."

"I, Tempest Danvers, promise to enter Fairy and help Julian Deveraux come back into Fairy so he gets everything he deserves on the stipulation that he leaves me and my kin alone once he crosses into Fairy."

My hand flamed red right before Julian's flamed blue. I shoved my hand into his, where the colors mingled to a light purple flame. Once the flame died down, Julian released my hand.

"There, the pact is final. I'll have Jax come up here and take you back to Fairy. I think you should make your way straight to The House of Autumn. Assuming nothing has changed in the last

300 years, your family's court is halfway between the Summer and Winter Courts, but if you stick to the trail, you should be able to avoid any royals from the Summer Court who might capture your heart."

I nodded before heading for the door. A pit of dread formed in my gut as I reached for the knob and without turning around, I said something which sounded more like a hopeful wish than anything. "I hope this works out so we can both get everything we deserve." I pulled open the door and exited, but I could have sworn I heard Julian mutter something that sounded like he planned on it.

Chapter 21

I stepped out into the hallway, taking a deep breath to steel myself. Waves of nausea churned in my stomach. I still wasn't sure this plan would work, but Julian had to pay for what he did to Maria. Part of me thought her death was now on my hands, since Julian believed she would spill her secrets to me. I allowed myself to become lost in thought as I made my way down to Jax's loft. He had agreed it would look more natural to anyone watching to meet him at the apartment before he took me to Fairy. *I was going to Fairy to claim ancient powers from who, my ancestors? A magic well? Was I losing my mind? Or maybe this was all a psychotic fever dream?*

Maria materialized next to me, walking beside me. I didn't notice until she spoke. "Tempy, you don't have to do this for me. It's not too late to back out."

I paused at Jax's door before looking up at her. "We have already struck the pact, Maria. I can't turn back at this point even if I wanted to. There is no way around this mess other than through it. We either succeed or, well, I don't know what."

"I'm sure if anyone could find a way, it would be you. But please, don't do this because you feel responsible for my death."

I gave my sister a sideways glance. "How'd you come to that conclusion?"

"Tempy, I know you and how your brain works. When Jax told you Julian thought I was working for you to undo him, I saw the look in your eyes. Don't you dare put my death on your shoulders. I may not remember a lot of what happened, but you had nothing to do with it. If I had never asked you to bring Julian to justice, you'd be at home writing another book and not risking your life to travel to some magical world."

I shook my head. "None of that matters now, Sis. I'll go into this Fairy place and do what I can."

The hairs on the back of my neck stood up, and I looked to my left to see a sparkling light. I gritted my teeth as the faint image of a man sparkled. I walked over to the sparkles and looked the ghost man dead in the eye. His eyes grew wide as he took a step back.

"Johnny, is it? You go on and run back to your master and tell him I'm doing what we agreed to. No need to follow me around."

The man's mouth opened and closed like a fish out of water. Sheer shock coloring his faint face. "You can see me?"

"I can now. Go on and git before I figure out how to rip you out of that plane and kill you all over again."

"Lady, I wish you would."

His words caused me to pause. "What does that mean? You don't like being Julian's eternal lacky?"

"It hurts to be in this existence. You're the first being outside of Julian I have been able to speak to since he did whatever this is to me. I just want to pass on, but he won't let me. All I want to do is rest, but I have to watch everyone out here living an endless soap opera. I'm tired."

Sadness washed over me. How could Julian be so damned cruel? "If I can free you, I will. Nobody deserves to stay in a state of unrest. Now, go on and tell Julian I left. OK?"

Johnny gave me a sad smile and nodded. "Thank you."

"Maria, you stay out here and make sure we don't have any other onlookers. I'll holler when we are about to leave so you can jump back into the necklace."

"No problem, Sis."

"What, no retort about talking to people who aren't there?"

Maria took her fingers and made a motion across her mouth like she was zipping her lips closed. "Nope, I'm getting used to your creepy powers to talk to imaginary people."

I suppressed a giggle before turning back around to raise my hand to knock when Jax's door suddenly flew open, causing me to lose my balance and crash into his chest.

"Ah, Tempest, glad to see you here. I have been told I am to escort you to Fairy. I was going to come pick you up from Julian's office."

The formal tone made me raise my brow. "Uhm, what?"

"Did Julian not explain the mission to you?"

"He did, but why are you talking like some weirdo with a stick up his behind?"

Jax sighed before dragging me into his apartment and closing the door. "What gives, Tempy? Do you want to blow our cover?"

I shrugged. "Er, I don't follow."

Jax leaned close to my ear and whispered. "Did you forget Johnny? He's probably watching and reporting back to Julian. Best he doesn't think we know each other."

I scoffed as I waved my hand. "Johnny? Yeah, I told him to take a hike and tell Julian I had left. He seems like a nice man caught in an impossible situation. He wants me to help free him, which I have added to my never-ending list of things Julian has broken, which I must fix."

Jax's eyes grew wide. Their amber color intensified for a split second before he opened his mouth. "Tempy, you can't see Johnny. That's the whole point of the ritual Julian put him through."

"Well, if Johnny is a man in his forties and dressed like an old-time mob boss, then yeah, I saw him. And he is miserable. I can't imagine having to wander around constantly on edge like Johnny has been having to do."

Shaking his head, a smile crept across Jax's face. "I guess this revelation shouldn't surprise me at this point. Follow me down the hallway and I'll take you to the portal."

I walked out the door behind Jax, picking up Maria on the way. Jax headed towards the weird dead-end hallway I hid his book in earlier in the week. "Seriously, the portal to a magical land is in an old snack alcove? I didn't see anything in there the other day."

Jax didn't slow his pace down as he spun around to face me. "You wouldn't have seen anything the day you stole the reports from my loft because you didn't know you could."

"Wait, you knew I took those papers? How?"

"I'd like to say I had a magical way to watch my place, but I saw you on the motion camera hidden on the shelf. It took several still pictures of you moving the box. When I got home and found the book gone, I figured you took both the book box and the papers. I confirmed my suspicions when I found said box empty inside this hallway. The fact you could enter the corridor is amazing and a testament to how powerful you may be."

I chewed my bottom lip as I followed Jax into the alcove. "So nobody else can see the hallway?"

"No, only Fae who know about Fairy can see the hallway."

We turned the little corner next to the table before I stopped mid-step. I gasped when I saw a wavy picture of a brightly lit field. "Woah, what the hell is that?"

"The Autumn Wheat Fields. They are right outside House Autumn's stronghold." Jax turned around, holding out his hand. "Take my hand so the portal doesn't play any tricks and separate us."

I laughed as I took the offered hand, allowing the sparks to flow into my arm. "Even the portals to Fairy are tricky?"

"Everything in Fairy is tricky, Tempy. Which is why I am going to help you. Just let me do all the talking. Let's go. Your destiny awaits."

Chapter 22

Jax pulled my hand as he stepped into the wavey light. I wasn't sure what to expect, but walking through the portal was a bit like walking out your front door. As soon as I placed my foot on the ground, my body warmed under the sparkling sun. A gentle breeze caressed my face. "Wow, it smells amazing here."

"Right now, The Summer Court is in control. In fact, it's been in control for the last two hundred years."

"That seems like a long time even for a magical land. Is that normal?"

"No, when The Summer Court came into its last rotation of power, they were supposed to name their successor. However, because of the curse, none of King Finvarra's sons had found a mate. No mates meant no new heirs. A Fae cannot take a throne without having an heir apparent. Thus, it's perpetually summer because we cannot hand off our rule to The Court of Autumn without naming our court's next ruler."

I tried to keep all the timelines straight in my head, but something felt off. Then I remembered my grandmother telling me something about when Jax was born. "My Gamma Tempest told me you were born two hundred years ago. I don't understand if the curse has been in effect for 300 years, how that could happen? Wouldn't the curse have stopped your birth?"

"They appointed King Finvarra before Oberon left for the mortal realm. Finvarra was only supposed to be an interim ruler. I guess Oberon believed he could come right back with Kinara in tow.

Of course, to be found worthy, Finvarra already had an established family. In fact, he was married to a Fae from The Autumn Court and together they had my eldest brother Asher."

A chill ran through my spine at my next thought. "Your mother is from House Autumn? Are we related, then?"

"My mother is not from House Autumn. I'm betting Julian already told you I was a bastard child and a pariah here in Fairy."

I looked down at my shoes. "He may have said something of your lineage."

"Part of what he told you is true. My mother is Queen of The Winter Court, but I am not as much of a pariah as Julian believes. That was part of my cover story, so he would trust me and see me as a double agent."

"Let me guess, King Finvarra found a loophole in the curse's wording?"

Jax smirked. "Something like that, but the truth is we don't know all the parts of the curse. We've discovered bits and pieces over the years, enough to know supposedly how to break the spell, but not all the details. I guess you could say I was an experimental child. My father's advisors decreed a child of Summer and Winter would break the curse. Unfortunately, what your Gamma noted about Fae mating under our laws being for life was true. My father didn't want to ruin any of his son's chances at a good relationship by forcing us to marry women from Winter. He held parties trying to find my eldest brother a compatible match, to no avail. Then one night The Summer Queen, Fay, took matters into her own hands. The Queen's own advisors thought Finvarra could produce a new heir from House Winter. Desperate to save her son's and her house's dignity, Fay drank a death potion. This left King Finvarra free of the life bond rule. He mourned Queen Fay for three days before the advisors brought the First Princess of the Winter Court to my father. Finvarra refused to wed the princess but took her as a consort instead. I was born not long after and as a reward for her service to the courts, they both agreed to elevate my mother, Morganna, to the position of The Queen of Winter. After her coronation, she abandoned me and never looked back."

"Jax, I don't know what to say. I'm sorry."

"I can't say I blame her after my father refused to wed her. Of course, Winter Fae are fickle creatures. Sometimes they joke a true Winter Fae has a heart made of ice."

"I'm guessing by the fact you were trying to marry me and break the curse, their plan didn't work?"

"I have had many Fae women paraded in front of me since I was thirty years old, which is a very young age for a Fae to begin dating. Father didn't wish to force a mate on me. Rather, he hoped someone would catch my eye and allow me to produce an heir. Alas, no one has ever captured my interest." Jax smirked before putting his hands in his pockets and looking away. "Well, except you, Tempest."

My face heated at Jax's last words. There was no way this was going to work. He couldn't be my guide as long as this curse was in effect, and I sure as hell didn't feel like marrying anyone. Taking in a deep breath, I looked up at Jax. "I'm sorry for this whole situation, Jax. Once I get my magic, I'll help find some alternative way to break the curse on The Court of Summer. If my ancestor cast part of the curse to begin with, surely I could break the spell."

"I'm glad to hear that, Tempy. Now, the first place we should check is the main dwelling for The Court of Autumn. We can reach it by traveling north towards the ridge there. The journey is about a thirty-minute hike from here."

I threw my hands up to stop Jax, careful not to touch him. "Jax, thank you for getting me this far. I appreciate your efforts. I am going to find these powers and help your family, but with this curse looming over everything, I think we should go our separate ways until I can claim my magic."

"No, Tempy! You don't have an inkling of the danger you put yourself in by not having a guide. Fairy is not a place from a children's book. It's a cruel realm, full of politics and tricks. Trust me, I grew up here. As long as we don't touch each other, I think we can keep our heads level enough to work together."

"I won't be alone, Jax. I'll have Maria with me. She may not be a Fae, but she can help me. Maybe she can find a nice Fae ghost to talk to."

Jax sighed as his shoulders slumped. "Tempest, listen to me, Maria wasn't from Fairy. She won't be able to help you here."

"I know she's not from Fairy, but she is resourceful. With her help, I am sure I can find my way. Now, if you will excuse me."

I turned to walk in the direction Jax had pointed out earlier. I made it about three steps before Jax's hand wrapped around my arm to drag me back. I let out a tiny moan as the electric contact I wasn't braced for zipped down my arm.

"Tempest, Maria can't help you because she can't manifest here. Maria was a human through and through and even though she is a ghost in a necklace, it doesn't change the fact she wasn't from this realm. Her essence isn't from here. The very fabric of Fairy renders a human ghost powerless even if their conduit is inside the realm."

"No, you must be wrong. I'll prove it." Grasping the necklace, I closed my eyes and willed Maria to appear. "Maria, I need you to come here, please."

I stood holding the necklace for what felt like forever, but Maria never came. Tears slid down my cheeks at being forced to relive the feeling of my sister's absence all over again.

"I'm sorry, Tempy. Humans can't be in Fairy, that's why if a Fae falls in love with a human, they have to stay in the human world to be with them."

"I'm human! Why am I able to come in here?"

A frown formed on Jax's face as he looked down at me. "Tempy, you are part Fae. Fairy recognizes you with your blood. Look, I know this is all shocking, but we are wasting time arguing over this. I will go with you and help you find your magic. At the end of the day, I'm your best bet as an ally. I understand how this place works and I do command some authority here. My mother may have abandoned me for a throne and I may be a bastard by your world's standards, but I still have royal blood in my veins."

Shaking my head, I pushed Jax away. "Maybe if Maria can't come, Gamma Tempest can come. She was a Fae."

"A Fae who never once set foot inside of Fairy. She wanted to live a simple life, remember?"

I squeezed my eyes closed. "But she knew you. How did she know you if she was never in Fairy!"

"After they deemed me a failure, I tried to go out into the mortal realm and find a Lost Daughter of Autumn. I was hoping to find a bride for my eldest brother. One of my first visits was with your grandmother. I tried to woo her into coming to Fairy, but she spat on my shoes. I attempted to keep tabs on her, but she was a master at cloaking. When I found her again, she was married to a human. I eventually gave up on her as a prospect when I realized she had birthed a son. Of course, about the same time as her rejection, I learned about Julian. I went back and reported the information I gathered to my father. And that is when he told me to befriend Julian and try to build a case against him."

A snot bubble formed at the end of my nose as my tears grew heavier. I had never felt so alone in my entire existence, not even after Maria died. Circumstances spared me from the heartache of losing my dad and grandmother because I didn't truly remember them. But after Maria died, I knew what loss felt like.

A hollow despair filled my belly as I stood ugly crying in the middle of a sunny field. I don't know how long I stayed there in my cold misery. I remained lost in a dark place in my mind where not even the glorious sun of Fairy could reach me. Finally, the pain ebbed away, but when I came back to, I found myself wrapped in Jax's arms. The fact his touch brought me out of my stupor miffed me, but this time, I didn't automatically push him away.

"We can stand here arguing about all of this and worrying about a curse none of us know all the parts to, or we can start walking towards the ridge to find your magic. But there is no way I'm leaving you alone inside Fairy. You'd be an easy target for so many things here, and I'm not just saying that because I need you to break a curse. Tempest Danvers, I like you a lot. I'd hate for you to get hurt because I let you push me away."

I rested my head on Jax's chest, trying to give myself a moment to recover. Maybe he was right. What the hell did I know about Fairy? Even if Maria or Gamma could help me, what did they know? I didn't want to play into the curse, but Jax was right about us not knowing all the parts of the spell. My resolve to find my magic alone waned. Without lifting my head, I nodded in agreement as I snaked my arms around his waist. Something felt so right about being in his arms, but until we broke this damned curse, I wouldn't ever be able to believe our feelings were genuine. I pushed up and away from Jax before walking towards the ridge. "Let's go before I change my mind."

Chapter 23

After traveling forever over rolling wheat fields, it became abundantly clear to me my boots were not, in fact, made for walking. "I thought you said this stronghold was only a thirty-minute hike. I feel like we've been walking for hours."

Jax chuckled as he stopped to look at me. "I take it you're not accustomed to hiking. We've only been moving for twenty-minutes. I haven't been to the stronghold of the Autumn Court for many years. For all I know, they moved the structure."

"What do you mean by moved? How do you move an entire court? Like, is it on wheels or something?"

"Seriously, Tempy? We are standing in a land called Fairy, and you think the Fae need wheels to move large objects?"

I gritted my teeth. *Of course, they would use magic. Duh, Tempy.* I balled my hands into fists before yelling at Jax. "Great, so we're lost out here wandering and it might take us another ten minutes or fifteen years? At this rate, Julian is going to die of old age before I can break any curses!"

"Stop being so dramatic, Tempy!" Jax kneeled and pointed to his back. "Here, get on my back and I'll carry you. I really think we will be there soon."

I rolled my eyes. "You would just love it if I rode around on your back, wouldn't you? Come on, I'm not falling for any of your woo-woo magic crap."

Jax stood up, raising an eyebrow while the corner of his mouth curled into a smirk. "Woo-woo magic crap? I assure you, if I were trying to seduce you, it would not involve a piggyback ride."

I let out a huff before shaking my head and stomping forward. The less I touched Jax, the less I would have that delicious curse induced electric shock coursing through my body. There was no way I was going to chance the curse sending me on my honeymoon because of a piggy-back ride. My mind ran around in circles, distracting me from my surroundings, and by the time I heard Jax yell, it was too late. A ball of energy plowed into me, knocking me onto my ass. Pain radiated through my body from whatever the hell that was. I struggled to sit up, but the world spun around me. I grasped my head and flopped back down on the ground.

"Tempest! Don't try to get up."

I heard Jax kneel next to me before his hands touched my face. This time there wasn't any kind of electric shock; instead, his hands radiated coolness against my rapidly heating cheeks. I tried to speak, but only mumbles came out.

"Shhh, Tempy... lay still while I draw the magic out of your body. If I don't pull it out, your brain will fry."

A cooling sensation washed over me, reducing the fire consuming my body. A wind tinged with the scent of fresh snow filled my nose. "Is it snowing?"

"Not quite. I'm using my Healing Snow magic to cool you down. A perk from my mother's line. Healing Snow will take a while to work, but it's the best thing I have to treat you with."

I giggled at Jax's response. I felt punch drunk and on fire all at the same time. "Can you build a snowman with your magic? Jax, build a snowman with me!"

"Shit, this is bad. Focus on my magic, Tempest. Feel the coolness wash through you and take away the heat. Don't let your mind wander too far off task."

The heat fought Jax's coolness, almost like the heat didn't want to submit to the cold. My head throbbed as I struggled to focus on Jax and his magic. I understood what was going on around me, but I couldn't form any coherent sentences. I tried to concentrate on Jax's face to will myself to do as he asked, but when I looked up, all I could see was an alien head growing out of Jax's shoulder. The eyes bulged out of a white, angular face framed by short white hair. I squinted, trying to figure out why Jax had a second head all of a sudden. "Hey Jax, why do you have an extra head?"

"Probably a fever dream, Tempest. If I can get this magic out of your body, you should recover. Just a few more minutes, OK? Please try to stay quiet."

"I thought we were here to put magic into my body. Maybe this is the magic I've been looking for? But damn it hurts."

Jax grimaced. "This is not your birthright, love. This is a battle spell which will kill you if I can't pull the essence out of your body. This is exactly why I didn't want you to go alone. You have no idea of the dangers in Fairy."

"Who shoots magic death balls out in the middle of a wheat field?"

"The Autumn Court guards. We must be closer than I thought to the front gates."

I lifted my hand to motion to my right. "Yeah, there is an enormous castle over there."

Jax looked up to where I pointed and frowned. "Tempy, there isn't anything there. Just lay still while I try to fix you."

"OK, fine. But could you do me a favor and tell your other head to go away? It's kinda freaking me out. Oh gawds, I won't grow an extra head when I get my magic, will I?" Without warning, Jax's second head smiled at me before hitting Jax over his first head, knocking him unconscious. This, in turn, caused me to let out a blood-curdling scream.

Jax's second head, which now had a lanky body attached, spoke to me. "Relax. Let me help you."

My eyes widened as the strange figure raised a sparkly staff in the air before swinging the weapon towards me. Instinct took over and I crossed my arms over my face to mitigate the impact. When the staff made contact, it wasn't a forceful blow. Rather more like a tickle, followed by a rush of coolness. Within seconds, I could sit up. I looked over at Jax and then up at the strange creature. "What the hell did you do to Jax?"

"I only knocked him out. He will come to in an hour or so."

Anger welled up coursing through my hands as I reared back to slug this person. "What right do you have to go around knocking people out? How the hell am I supposed to find my way around this godforsaken land without my guide!"

The figure stepped to the side, allowing my fist to whiz right past them. "Is this how you treat your savior? I would expect you to be more grateful to be free of Jax."

Exasperated, I threw my hands up in the air. "What in the world are you talking about? Jax brought me here to help me."

The figure stood still, leaning on their staff with an emotionless face. "You mean he brought you here to force you to marry him?"

"Let me make something perfectly clear. I, Tempest Danvers, am not marrying anyone. No one is forcing me to marry them. I'm not dating anyone. So, no, Jax and I are not a couple."

"So, if you are not intending to marry Jax, why are you here with him then, Lost Daughter of House Autumn?"

I crossed my arms and scowled at the strange, lanky creature. "How do you know I am a Lost Daughter of House Autumn?"

"Your human side reeks and you can see me. Only those with the blood of the Autumn Court can see through our cloaks. Therefore, your friend could not see me or the stronghold. Again, I ask you why you are here if not to marry Jax and break the curse?"

I stood straight and clicked my tongue before answering the figure. "Simple. I'm here to claim my magic."

Chapter 24

I stood staring as this strange figure doubled over, howling in laughter before me. The short, white hair bobbed with each giggle as the creature gasped for air. "That's the best joke I've heard in a long time!"

"This wasn't a joke. I traveled here with Jax to accept the magic I am due from The Court of Autumn and break these stupid curses once and for all."

The figure stilled as it returned staring at me, no longer laughing. It raised its hand and then pointed at itself. "I am Nara, Guard of The House of Autumn. I would like to tell you there was something for you here, but we have no magic to give you."

"That's impossible! Do you want me to prove myself or something before you show me where the magic is? Don't you want this curse to end? Wouldn't you like summer to conclude? I mean I like nice weather as much as the next, but hundreds of years of summer? Hard pass."

Nara sighed as she shook her head. "I don't know who led you to believe there was magic for you to accept, but there is nothing here. This curse has bound all The House of Autumn's magic. We barely survive with our innate magic, let alone have any to spare. You've made a trip to this land for nothing."

"I refuse to believe this is a wasted trip. Can't you take me into the stronghold and let me at least look around? Maybe Jax and I could find something you have overlooked."

Nara stamped her staff onto the ground and pointed at Jax. "This whelp cannot enter our sacred home."

I looked at Nara and then to Jax. "I can't leave him out here in the middle of a field unconscious. I need his help. Maybe he can come in as my guest. I mean, he is out of it right now. What harm can he cause?"

"No, we will never allow this bastard into our sacred home. His birth caused our dear Fay's death."

"You can't blame Fay's death on Jax. She killed herself of her own accord before Jax was born. Seems to me you should honor her sacrifice a little better. From what I hear, Fay did what she thought what was right to save her people."

"Her death was a meaningless loss, as we are still cursed." Nara turned to walk back towards the stronghold.

"Are you sure? If Jax wasn't around, do you think I'd be standing here? Maybe a child of Summer and Winter breaking the curse means Jax would find me in the human realm and bring me back to Fairy?"

Nara spun around and laughed. "And what will your watered-down Fae blood do for House Autumn? You certainly have the arrogance of a human thinking you could come here and fix anything."

"Whatever. The curse seems to imply no Lost Daughter of House Autumn will ever return to Fairy, but here I am. I came here of my own free will to claim my birthright. So, you can either help me and Jax into the stronghold or not. Doesn't matter to me either way, because I'm going to find this magic."

"I will not be the one to help you, nor will I allow you into our stronghold. Go back to your human life."

I stood planted in the ground as Nara turned away again. Another figure, not as lanky as Nara, walked towards me. I wasn't sure where she came from, but she walked right past Nara, not giving her a second look. The honey-blonde woman stopped in front of me and bowed.

"Please excuse my sister's anger. She takes her post to guard our court from harm a little too serious. I can help you take Jax to the stronghold if you would like."

"How are we going to get Jax all the way over there? He weighs a ton, and I can't drag him."

The woman smiled. "No worries. I can transport him with my magic."

The stranger waved her hand, and the next thing I knew, Jax was floating behind her. My mouth hung open as she walked away.

"If you don't follow me, you are liable to have bees set up in your mouth, dear."

I snapped back to reality, telling myself this was all real and I shouldn't be in shock at seeing magic. I mean, I walked through a wall in a snack alcove to get here. "Right, sorry. Uhm, what was your name?"

"You can call me Lady. Now, follow me and I'll take you to the library archives in the heart of our stronghold. There you will find everything you need."

Lady and I walked next to each other, but I kept checking on Jax to make sure she didn't drop him along the way. I wasn't sure what I would find in the library, but at least I was going to get into the stronghold. I was looking forward to finding furniture where I could sit down and rest my aching feet. The blister forming on my heel made itself known by shooting a pain through my right foot. For supposed authentic combat boots, their manufacturing was shoddy. How could soldiers march in these things?

We inched closer to the stronghold, which looked more like an oddly shaped castle. Instead of square corners, the outline of the building had a curved appearance. There was no visible door, but there was a winding exterior staircase and a few tall windows. Next to what I assumed was the main part of the castle was a large, rounded stone with grass on the top. The whole design was odd. I don't know what I was expecting to find in a land of magic, but it wasn't this.

Lady stopped right outside one of the curving staircases and waved her hands. A mass of small trees stood up, revealing an entrance. Lady walked through, towing Jax behind her. I stood inspecting the trees, fully expecting them to smack me when I tried to go inside the doorway.

"Come along, Tempest Danvers. You can't face your destiny out here in the stairwell."

I gulped down a few breaths of air before forcing my body forward to catch up with Lady. I followed her up the stairway around to the back of the building. There we came face to face with a gilded door. Jewels set into the gold sparkled, making a mosaic of a fall scene full of red and vibrant orange trees. Lady waved her hand causing the doors to swing open.

Stepping through the door, I gasped as I looked up seeing the dome-like ceiling. Jeweled leaves twinkled all throughout the autumn forests depicted in the scenes. As my gaze moved around the room, I focused on the walls, seeing row after row of books running from the floor to the ceiling. Each level of shelving had a platform in front which curved up and led into the next level of books. "Wow, that's a lot of books."

Lady levitated Jax over to a comfy looking chaise, depositing his still body before walking back towards me where I stood gawking like an idiot.

"Alright, dear. This is the heart of our stronghold. Here you will find a superior collection of history, magic, and informational books. You are free to look around and investigate anything you feel pulled towards. With any luck, your companion will awaken soon and can assist you."

"What do I do if someone comes in here and asks me what I am doing? I mean, if Nara comes in here, won't she want to zap me with a death ball again?"

Lady smiled. "All you need to do is tell them Lady let you into the library and gave you permission to search for your magic. Go on, dear, you have many nooks and crannies to check."

I nodded before looking back towards the books. While taking a deep breath, I ran my fingers through my hair. I groaned out loud as I didn't have a clue where I was going to find this magic or even where to start. I was hoping this would be a show up, pass go, and collect some magic kind of deal. Lady was nowhere to be found when I turned around to ask her something. Feeling rather deflated, I walked towards the shelves of books. Not having a better idea, I started at the beginning and ran my fingers over every single book, praying my intuition or something would help me out.

The bookshelves reached thirty feet off the ground, with no way for me to safely climb up to touch all the books. Stretching my aching arms and neck, I looked at the rest of the room. Surveying the space from where I stood, searching for anything that could help me. For support, I leaned on the banister. I noticed Jax still passed out on the chaise but sighed in relief to see we were still alone in this room. My gaze raked across the room towards a darkened corner. I stared at the darkness for a moment and swore there was a little golden sparkle over there. Making a mental note of what row I was on, I made my way down the platform and towards the sparkling light.

I crossed the room, passing the chaise Jax occupied. I stopped briefly to make sure he was still breathing. Noticing the rise and fall of his chest, I went back to moving towards the mysterious, flashing sparkles. Oddly enough, when I got to the corner, it was as if the books on the shelf were blocked by a cloud of ink colored smoke. I couldn't make out any of the titles. My hand seemed to disappear into the heavy shadow hovering over the books. Frowning,

I pulled my hand back inspecting myself for damage. Deciding to trust the sparkling light, I shoved my hand back into the darkness at the spot where the light originated. I wrapped my fingers around an enormous book and pulled. Electricity buzzed through my hand. Ignoring the tingle, I proceeded to pull out my prize.

Once free of the inky darkness, I realized the tome was a massive, leather-bound volume covered in golden swirls. The book reminded me of the ones villains used in kid's movies. I lugged it over to a table for a more thorough inspection. My heart fell when I saw the title written in some weird language. Running my fingers over the title, a name appeared in my mind. *Necromancer's Guide to Ancestry.* The sudden realization of the title popping up in my mind caused me to freak out a tiny bit. *Holy shit! How did I know the name of the book? I don't know this language.*

Opening the manuscript, I flipped through several chapters. Brushing my fingers over the ancient appearing script, I watched as the strange language re-arranged itself on the pages to appear written in English. I was so enamored with the automatic translation I didn't notice when someone walked into the library.

"What are you doing here? How did you access this sacred space?"

I looked up to find Nara scowling at me. I stood straighter and squared my shoulders before answering. "Lady brought me here and gave me permission to research."

Nara's face fell as I saw her cheeks redden. "Who the hell told you about Lady? Is this some kind of sick joke?"

Perplexed, I raised my hands. "No, she really led me here. She helped me transport Jax."

"Unbelievable. First you bring the outcast Summer bastard here and then you have the audacity to invoke the name of one of my dearest friends to prove you have permission to be here. No, you need to leave, now!"

Noticing Lady walk into the room, I raised my hand and pointed. "Why don't you ask Lady herself?"

"You must have a crack in your pot! Talking to Lady is impossible."

"OK. I don't see how. I mean, she's standing right there next to you. You can't just ask her?"

Lady smiled at me. "Tempest, turn to page 356 of the book you are reading. I want you to read what's on the page out loud."

I shrugged, choosing to humor Lady. I found page 356 and touched the spell. As soon as my fingers lifted from the page, the words translated into English. I silently read the spell before raising a brow. "Are you sure you want me to read this, Lady?"

Nara scoffed as she stalked towards me with her staff raised. "Stop acting like you are talking to Lady!"

"Tempest, read the incantation now, please!" Lady yelled.

"See what was lost. Come forth in my pain. Let me forget ye not."

As soon as the words left my mouth, the room exploded into a bright light, blinding me and I hoped Nara. I wasn't sure how a spell that blinded me would help smooth things over with Nara. Then I heard Lady shouting.

"Nara! Turn around and face me."

Nara's eyes opened wide as she slowly turned around to look at who was yelling. "Laa...Lady? How can you be here? What kind of evil spell is this?"

"Calm down, Nara, and stop being so dramatic. I'm always here. You just haven't been able to see me. Your grief blinds you from my presence. Two-hundred years is a long time to lament. Don't you think it's about time to get over the choice I made? I didn't take my life in vain. He has brought her here."

"I refuse to believe this conjure! You are saying what the human wills you to say. These lies are what she also spouted. Jax is a traitor by birth and your death has brought us nothing but grief. Our magic is bound, and our people suffer. Sister, why did you do this to us?"

"Nara, you did this to yourself. The heavy cloud of grief permeating this place keeps your magic bound, and it keeps me here. And if Jax was a mistake, how did he find the heir? That girl can pierce the veil with her innate magic. How do you think she saw the stronghold or me? She cast a powerful necromancy spell right before your eyes, even so, you refuse to accept the truth. Nara, you need to do your duty. Show her the jewel of House Autumn."

Nara crossed her arms. "If I refuse?"

"She'll find it eventually, but if you want our people's suffering to end sooner rather than later, help her."

Nara fell to her knees and sobbed before Lady.

Things finally started adding up. "I take it your name isn't Lady. More like Queen Fay, am I right?"

Lady smiled. "You catch on quick. There may be hope for this curse to be broken at last."

Chapter 25

"Stand up, little sister, and help Tempest unlock the magic she came here for. Fulfill your duty to our people and help the heir. She has many trials still before she can succeed. We have no time to waste."

Nara stood back up and wiped the tears off her face. "As you wish, sister."

Lady smiled before her image flickered. "Thank you, Nara. Now, I can finally rest."

"Wait, don't leave me!" Nara ran up to Lady, attempting to grasp onto her form, but her arms swooshed through Lady's body.

"I have to go for you to grow into your role as leader. Once Tempest lifts the curse, our people will need you to usher them into the new era."

"I am not ready, Lady!"

"Yes, you are, Nara. You were born ready. You are the next Queen of The Autumn Court. Now, hold your head up high and remove that awful glamour. You are no longer a child."

Nara nodded to Lady before shaking her head. Her once short, white hair dissolved into long, honey-blonde hair. The spell replaced the sickly pallor she sported with a golden skin. "Goodbye, Lady. May you finally rest in the great beyond."

I eyed Nara warily as she turned. The angular face she once sported was now replaced with one which looked like Lady's. A smile formed on her lips before she nodded to me.

"If you follow me, I will take you to the chamber where we keep the Wheat Stone."

I looked at Nara and then at Jax. "Will he be alright there? Nobody will hurt him, will they?"

"For someone who does not wish to marry Jax, you sure worry about him. No matter, he will be fine here. No one will come here and if they did, they would never attack royalty."

"Then why did you attack him?"

"I merely knocked him out for a bit. Tempest, I promise you, no one will cause Jax any harm. Once you have returned from the chamber, he should be awake. Now come, we don't have time to waste." Nara turned and walked towards a circle in the middle of the library. She stood on an intricate pattern of woven grape vines before flicking her fingers. At her command, part of the floor sank down, revealing a stairway leading down into a chamber.

I gulped at the darkness below us as a sense of ominous dread crawled up my spine.

A smirk played across Nara's lips. "The passage will illuminate as we walk. The sacred treasure is in the center of the chamber."

I followed Nara down what felt like five hundred steps, and as promised, the path lit up, ensuring I never felt like I was waltzing into my grave. Once we reached the last step, an altar greeted us in the center of the room. Floating above the altar was some kind of glowing medallion-looking thing. I could only assume the object was this Wheat Stone Nara had mentioned. Nara walked up to the platform and bowed.

I felt out of place in the weird chamber and for the first time since crossing into Fairy I had no clue how I needed to proceed. "So, uh, what do I do now?"

"You must solve the riddle of the stone to unlock your ancestral magic."

I frowned. "I'm not good at puzzles."

Nara shrugged. "Then I guess you came here for nothing. It's a shame you have given up before you have cast a thorough gaze upon the sacred treasure."

I huffed out a sigh and moved closer to the altar. Peering at this so-called sacred object, I realized someone set the stone in an ornate metal disc. I reached out my hand, pulling down the disc, inspecting the item. Intricate patterns etched into the metal intertwined to form a depiction of wheat around a red jewel in the center.

Inside the large disc were four other discs, all equidistant from one another. I flipped the object over to find the back made from plain, hammered metal. When I spun the disc around in my hand again, one of the four circles on the front jiggled. Drawing my bottom lip into my mouth, I contemplated how to unlock the puzzle.

The longer I held onto the disc, the calmer I grew in feeling. After a few minutes of staring and thinking, a cool breeze washed over me. The smell of leaves filled my nose, causing me to close my eyes and inhale deeply. I grabbed my necklace, wishing my sister could come here. "Oh Maria, where are you with your funny words when I need you?" I laughed as a memory came to my mind. I shrugged at the audacity of the situation before concentrating and speaking the words. "Mots Magiques."

No sooner had the words left my lips, the discs on the items spun around in rapid motion. Each disc picked up speed to where the larger disc began shaking in my hand. Hot energy poured down both of my arms, resulting in a searing pain, but I refused to drop the disc. The jewel in the center glowed orange, bathing me and the room in its light. I held onto the object for dear life until finally a zap traveled down my spine. At the same time, I heard a popping noise echo in the chamber. The feelings washing over me were alien, like something sinewy taking up residence in my spine while simultaneously slithering down my arms. A shudder moved through my body, resulting in my finally dropping the disc.

I looked up at Nara. Her face drawn in horror as she ran to scoop up the Sacred Treasure I'd just dropped. She examined the object before raising her head to glare at me with tear-filled eyes. "You've cracked The Wheat Stone!"

I stood in the center of this strange room, unsure of what to say. The once orange stone was now a dull, cracked white. "I don't understand. I said the first thing which came to mind." A wave of nausea crashed over me. I doubled over in pain, clutching at my sides. "Why does this hurt? What the hell is happening to me?" Another pain hit and this time I sank to my knees.

"You have betrayed us all! This stone was the only thing allowing our people to survive. You've drained The Wheat Stone of all its magic. You have doomed us!" Nara wailed.

Fire coursed through my body as the air became too thick to breathe. Kneeling on the floor, I panted, trying to fight the pain. A million hot razor blades ripped through my very being while Nara stood there cursing at me. I just needed to catch my breath, but whatever was happening to me was wreaking major havoc on my body. I closed my eyes, letting the pain take me under. Maybe oblivion was the better option. I sank lower into myself, losing all connection with the outside world, until cool hands touched my cheeks. The raging fire in my body ebbed, chased by an autumn wind and the scent of leaves. I could hear people talking, but it didn't make any sense.

A familiar male voice filled my mind. *Did those icy winds belong to Jax?*

"Tempy! Don't succumb to oblivion and don't let the pain fool you. The magic, it's testing you."

But why was the magic testing me? Didn't it belong to me?

With that thought, an alien voice invaded my mind. "You must earn the magic of the ancestors, Tempest Danvers."

I felt my brow crease. "How does one earn this magic? I don't understand. I only came for my trapped magic. Not some conglomeration of ancestral power."

The disembodied voice laughed. "The magic belongs to all the Lost Daughters of House Autumn born outside of Fairy. You must prove your body is worthy of being a vessel for this intense magic. It rebuilds you from the inside out. Survive the process, Lost Daughter, and we shall reward you."

"And what happens if I fail?"

"You die and we rebuild the Wheat Stone with your essence, just as it has been for hundreds of years."

"I'm not the first to come back, am I?"

"No, there were many others. They were weak."

Anger rose in my being at the response of the voice. "Is this a game to you? I didn't come here to die."

"No one ever intends to die. They only want the power. Mostly for themselves."

I tried taking in deep breaths. This voice was taunting me. Was this part of the rebuilding process? Nothing made sense. Unless there was more to the curse? "Who are you?"

A giggle and snicker echoed in my mind. "Not a who, but a what."

"Damn it, can nothing be straightforward with you Fae!"

"When is a curse, not a curse? When it becomes sentient."

"You're trying to tell me you are the curse made flesh?"

The voice changed from a light giggle to a deep, ominous tone. "Clever girl. There may be hope for you yet."

I grew tired of the games, which were literally in my head. "Enough! My name is Tempest Danvers, and I am here to break this curse on all sides. I will no longer allow hundred-year-old Fae politics to run amok in the human realm! Nor will a crazy fever dream hinder me. I am taking back all of House Autumn's lost magic. Julian Deveraux will cross into Fairy, and I will free The Court of Autumn from the yoke of this marriage curse. I will crush you, whatever you are!"

My body filled with conviction, quenching the fire. Using my mind, I pushed all the golden light snaking around my body back into the outside world. I felt another snap in my spine, followed by a fizzle, which reminded me of a puff of smoke. I felt more like myself and less like an addled, feverish lunatic.

Once the nausea subsided, I opened my eyes. I was no longer in the chamber, but I was lying on a chaise with Jax cradling my body while he wiped a cool cloth over my forehead. I studied Jax for a moment. He appeared lost in thought as he worked to wipe my head. His expression was somber. A smile formed on my lips as I realized he was worried about my wellbeing.

Even though I was awake and apparently alive, it didn't help ease the pain. I still felt like a truck ran over my very soul. Unfortunately, there was no time for a pity party. I could feel Julian crossing the border into Fairy at this very moment. We needed to be ready. I had doubts about Julian coming into Fairy. I looked up at Jax. "Hey, pretty boy, are you ready?"

Jax sighed. "Thank goodness, Tempy. I thought I lost you. What happened?"

"I did mind battle with an ancient, sentient curse and I won."

Jax's brow crinkled and I knew he was about to start asking a million questions.

Feeling better by the minute, I smiled as I threw up my hands, cutting Jax's question off. "Hush, we have plenty of time for questions later. I broke the curse preventing Julian from coming here. He just crossed into Fairy. We need to get into position. I know he's headed straight for your father and The Summer Court."

Chapter 26

Thanks to Jax's magic, we arrived in The Summer Court before Julian, but I knew we wouldn't have much time. While the rest of my body hummed with nervous energy, the unease in my gut intensified. They set the Summer Court in a beautiful plein air area. They marked the four corners of the space with oak trees instead of pillars. Rows upon rows of blossoming trees lined the outside area, creating a living wall while providing some privacy from the outside world. In the area's heart stood an ornate chair carved into the shape of a gigantic oak tree. The branches of the tree chair stretched upwards about five feet. I squinted to see the details, but I could have sworn the tree chair had real leaves.

I remained off to the side of the outdoor area under one of the pink, blooming trees. Petals from the flowers on the trees rained down on me, releasing a fragrant perfume smell. The air was heavy with the smell of fresh rain and roses. Jax stood talking to his father, King Finvarra, while also flinging his arms around him. I stood so far back I couldn't make out what they were discussing because Jax thought it would be better for him to speak to his father first.

I didn't know the layout of Fairy or the distance from the portal Julian took to where we were, but I could feel him nearing the court at an increased pace. Pushing myself off the tree, I approached Jax. I tried to avoid catching King Finvarra's attention, but his eyes kept drilling a hole through me. Ignoring the King's gaze, I touched Jax's arm. "Jax, Julian is closing in on us at an increased rate. I think he's regained some of his power. We need to be ready for him."

Jax nodded while his father continued to bore holes through my soul. I avoided direct eye contact with Finvarra, but when he growled while tossing his golden locks behind him, I felt myself looking up into his eyes.

Finvarra crossed his arms when he realized he had my attention. "Do you know the danger you have placed Fairy in? Of all the selfish things. To let Julian back into Fairy!"

I raised my brow before laughing. "You have to be kidding me, right? We both know Julian was always going to get back into Fairy once I came here. I am a Lost Daughter of House Autumn and coming here by my choice breaks the curse my ancestor uttered. So instead of bickering with Jax over the finite details, how about we prepare to enact the plan where Julian reaps what he has sown?"

Finvarra's jaw tightened. "That's exactly the issue here, Miss Danvers. Jax should have never encouraged this reckless plan. It shouldn't surprise me that my failure of a son would bring about the fall of House Summer."

Jax took a step back. "Father, what are you talking about? We can break the curses and be free of this drudgery. I thought you'd be happy to hear of the progress."

A voice came out from the grove of trees to the left. "Oh, Jax, you are more naïve than I guessed."

I turned to find Julian approaching our group. Even though he looked more like a Fae here in Fairy, glowing and radiant as a summer sun, the sight of him still repulsed me. You can wrap up dirt in a pretty container as much as you want, but at the end of the day, it's still dirt. The gnawing something was wrong in the pit of my stomach grew with each step he took towards us. By the time Julian stood next to me, I felt nauseated.

Julian bowed before taking my hand. I struggled to break away from him, but his grip was ironclad. "Julian, you're hurting my hand. Let go."

Julian smirked while he continued to hold my hand. Finally, he let my hand drop before facing King Finvarra and bowing. "My liege, I am glad to see you are well. I see the House of Summer has amassed many treasures since I last saw you. How does Queen Fay fair?"

Finvarra snarled at Julian before glancing over at Jax. "She's dead, but I suspect you know this."

Julian stepped back and bowed. "I am sorry. I did not know she had passed. What ailed her? Tree rot? Root breaks?"

Finvarra flung his hands out in front of him as his face turned red. "Enough! Drop the charade. What do you want?"

Julian looked over at me and smiled before turning back to Finvarra. "My liege, I only want what I deserve, which is vengeance against my oppressor."

Finvarra raised a brow while stroking his beard. "Who do you wish to have vengeance against?"

Julian lifted his finger and pointed the slender digit directly at me. "Tempest Danvers of House Autumn. Although not directly responsible, she is the only living relative in the direct bloodline of Kinara, thus under Fae law, she is responsible."

Heat flashed through me as my hands clenched into fists. "We had a deal, Julian! You sealed this deal with a Fae pact. Or was that just another one of your games?"

Julian let out a bellow of a laugh. "Dear, sweet Tempest, how clueless you are when it comes to the pacts Fae make. Yes, Julian struck an actual bargain with you in the world of humans. You'd break the spell, and he'd leave you alone."

I didn't let Julian finish. I cut him off as anger snaked throughout my body. "Right, so what is this bullshit where you're trying to punish me?"

"The minute I walked through the portal back into Fairy I was no longer Julian. I reclaimed my birthright, which is the name

Oberon, and all the power which goes with my true name. So, it is not Julian who is accusing you of wrongdoing, but rather Oberon."

"Why are you splitting hairs? You and I made a deal, and you are trying to back out on the agreed-upon terms!" My fists glowed as my body temperature rose. I gritted my teeth to bite back the explosion of power wanting to burst out of my arms. The more I seethed, the hotter I felt. I raised my arm and closed my eyes. I encouraged the magic to obey me, and for a moment, I felt the power surface. Each second passing caused me to lose more control. I saw myself blowing up Julian with a golden ray of light. The power almost reached my fingertips when I felt a pair of arms wrap around my waist, filling me with a cool breeze.

Jax leaned close to my ear as he pulled my arm down to my side. "I told you he was tricky, Tempy. Using your powers here will only lead to you being executed. He isn't just Julian anymore. He's Oberon, the Cursed King of Summer, and he has returned to Fairy. We have to let him speak, but let me handle your defense."

Julian turned to look at me and Jax before sneering. "You see, King Finvarra? She is dangerous! It's only your bastard son who can control this power-hungry mixed blood."

Finvarra sighed before clapping his hands. A surge of energy went through the air, and before I could blink, he conjured two stands of people on either side of the court area. "Enough, Oberon! Stick to your complaint and present us with the information."

"Your majesty, I was wrongly cursed by that girl's bloodline. The things I have done have only been to survive, and I broke no rules of Fairy in doing so. I was cut off, exiled, and dethroned all because I wanted what I was promised. They pledged Kinara to me, and she brought dishonor on the House of Autumn by doing what she did. And then to curse me on top of everything? I was king! Such blatant disobedience from a resident of Fairy cannot go unpunished. This girl isn't completely without fault, either. Tempest Danvers used both me and your son to get back into Fairy. She made promises which she had no intention of fulfilling. It saddens me to see Jax so in love with a crafty character. She reminds me so much of Kinara. Do you know Tempest broke my curse first because she wanted to be with me? She knows I am the rightful King of The Summer Court and thought bringing me back to my throne would grant her a place by my side. One thing I have learned, Tempest Danvers of House Autumn only desires power. She has no care for our laws and traditions. She made a pact with Jax, leading him to believe she would break the curse on The Summer Court. Please, King Finvarra, I only ask to receive a just judgement."

Rage filled my being. My jaw clenched as I gritted my teeth to keep quiet. Jax kept a firm hold on me, preventing me from moving. Julian stood there before a court of Fairy lying about everything. Fire snaked through my body. Gamma Tempest was right; this Fae was slippery. I can see now why Kinara rejected this jerk and cursed him. I reached up to clutch my necklaces tight in my hand, biting my tongue and praying King Finvarra would see through the deception.

"These are some serious accusations, Oberon. You are expecting me to believe this young woman who grew up in the land of humans learned enough magic to carry on a three-hundred-year-old curse?"

"She was not alone, my liege. She had help. Did you know this woman sent her sister to spy on me? Tempest and her sister worked to entrap me in some illegal scheme to hurt our Pixie allies. I was utterly devastated at finding out about being conned. Maria was my fiancée. I loved her, but I love Fairy and our laws more. Which is why I killed Maria, who was a full human and knew about Fae. No one else could have told Maria about Fae affairs other than Tempest. She's nothing more than a Lost Daughter of House Autumn perpetrating her ancestor's desire for chaos."

Julian winked at me when he finished twisting reality in front of everyone. But at the mention of my sister and the admission of her death as if it were an everyday occurrence, my resolve to bite my tongue broke. Clutching my sister's necklace, I felt my magic welling up inside, snaking out from my heart and down my arm. Ancient spells filled my mind as I concentrated my will on making Maria able to speak to refute these baseless accusations. Heat welled at the end of my fingers as a smoke-like substance poured out of my hand. Searing pain shot through me, causing me to yell out. All the eyes in the Summer Court turned towards me while watching the shape of a woman's form materialize from the smoke pouring out of my hands. With each passing second, Maria's form became clearer until my sister stood in the middle of Fairy. Jax gasped before backing away from me while I collapsed on the ground.

Chapter 27

Chaos broke out, drowning out King Finvarra's voice shouting for order. Guards appeared and attempted to detain Maria, but my magic wrapped itself around her keeping her safe. I felt drained and shaky, but I stood back up to stare at the image of my sister made flesh again. I walked towards her and tried to speak, but all the noise of the uproar drowned out her voice. Another flash of anger welled within me. Didn't they know I was trying to speak to my sister? Something bubbled up from deep inside me, causing me to yell. "Silence!" My voice boomed over the court, echoing through the valley and causing several nearby rocks to split.

A look of panic and shock fell over the bystanders, but I kept moving towards my sister. I held out my hands to take hers, shaking my head the entire time. "Maria? Is it you? Are you real?"

"Seriously, Tempy, you doubt I'm real! Aren't you the girl that talked to ghosts for a living before coming to a mythical land called Fairy to claim her Fae birthright? I mean, I just appeared out of the ends of your fingers after being stuck in my necklace for almost a year, for crying out loud! You can't make this stuff up!"

I threw my arms around Maria and sobbed. She felt as solid as anyone else. "I don't understand. How are you here?"

Maria stepped back and patted me on the shoulders. "I'm only here because I need to tell the truth about Julian. I can't stay like this for long, but I intend to fix this mess so I can finally rest. Your magic helped me form here in Fairy."

My head slumped. "But what about your memories? I thought Julian scrambled your brain?"

"Yeah, he thought that too, but turns out, as soon as your magic brought me back, it removed the blocks he'd placed. I remember everything. Even things I didn't know I should remember. We've got this. Now introduce me." Maria winked at me before giving me a gentle nudge towards King Finvarra.

"King Finvarra, I contest Julian Deveraux's complaint. The only true thing he has said in the last few moments is that he killed my very human sister, Maria Cardinal, because she saw things she should not have seen. And to prove it, I present to you my sister Maria."

An excited buzz rushed through the onlookers as Maria approached the King. There were words thrown around like necromancer and veil piercer. I tried to block them out. I was still in shock about Maria being there in front of me again after all this time. Perhaps I was really passed out on the floor of my house, overcome with grief. My powers being some metaphor for how I wish I could reach into death itself and pluck her soul back to the land of the living. OK, maybe I had read one too many supernatural novels.

King Finvarra squinted at Maria before nodding. "Well, tell us your story, human. But make it quick. Entertaining the thoughts of a human, especially one brought here by necromancy, is highly unusual."

Maria nodded. "My name is Maria Cardinal, and Julian Deveraux killed me because I discovered he was smuggling Pixies to be sold on the black meat market. It shouldn't matter if his name is Julian or Oberon. Regardless, this man standing here was my fiancé, and he killed me."

"Lies! Surely, you cannot allow a necromantic abomination to argue against me. This thing is obviously under Tempest's control. She doesn't look like my late fiancée."

"Oh, I can prove I'm the real deal and not under Tempy's control. There's a book in my old loft. It's behind a false panel in my closet. I knew this hiding place would go unnoticed by Julian because he didn't give a damn about my clothes. He only wanted to use me and my success to smuggle those poor Pixies to other supernaturals living abroad in a meal delivery service. You'll find details, pictures, and recordings. Julian thought he erased my memories. He thought he got all the evidence I had collected too, but I counteracted his mind magic. I rescued a Pixie, and she helped me by enchanting my necklace against his mind wipes. She wanted me to work with Jax to bring Julian down. You'll find her full written confession in the evidence I have. Send someone for the book, and I am sure the evidence will be compelling."

Finvarra frowned, stroked his beard, and grumbled out loud. "Jax! Is anything this thing says true? You were there, but I don't recall you ever telling me of these facts."

"Father, I don't know what Maria is talking about. I wasn't aware of her investigative endeavors. I can neither vouch for nor refute her allegations."

"Utter ridiculousness! You are more of a failure than I suspected. It was your job to gather the information to build the case against Julian. And you are telling me a mere human gathered intel you can neither deny nor verify? I thought she was your human contact!"

Jax stood tall, squaring his shoulders. "I was building a solid case against Julian. I have evidence of his wrongdoings. However, Julian manipulated Maria's memories many times before she came to me with her concerns. This evidence could be something she had, but didn't think she could share with me until I gained her trust. I know Julian killed Maria and justified the act with Fae law."

The King shook his head before sitting back down in his tree throne and lifting his hands to massage his temples. "Bring me the Orb of Seeing and a Courier, now! I want the Courier to enter the human world and find this supposed evidence. Bring whatever is found back here, and I will have Lord Anders authenticate the evidence. For now, we will have a brief recess. We will begin again once the Courier and the Orb of Seeing have returned with the purported evidence."

Maria strode over to Julian before drawing her arm back and smacking him. The sound of flesh colliding into flesh echoed in the air. Another round of gasps came from the onlookers in the stands. Guards rushed towards Maria, and I instinctively pushed my magic around her. The two guards bounced off my magic barrier a few times before giving up.

Julian's face darkened before being led away, escorted by the two guards. I held my breath as she walked over to where I stood.

Maria smiled, flashing her teeth. "Well, that's twice I've witnessed people bounce off me through some invisible force. I have a sneaking suspicion this is your handy work, Tempy."

"Maybe, I don't know for sure. This magic differs from the minor spells I did back home. Plus, I've only had these powers for a few hours. I just know when I see anyone getting close to you, I want to keep them away."

Maria snickered while she placed an all too real feeling hand on my shoulder. "Oh Tempy, I think you know more than you let on about the magic you've collected."

I scowled before chewing the inside of my cheek. What was that supposed to mean? Maria couldn't know what I saw during my battle with the curse, could she? "Let's pretend I don't know. What do you think I should know?"

"You forget, Sis, I'm always with you. I was there watching you battle for your magic, though I couldn't manifest here in Fairy. I don't understand exactly what I heard the energy entity tell you, but I know there is more to the curse than what your grandmother or Jax knew."

I let out my breath. "Unfortunately, I think I understand exactly what the being was trying to tell me, but at this point, I don't understand why. For right now, I am going to concentrate on getting Julian, or whatever his name is now, punished for your murder. I can't hope these Fae will punish him for a human death, but if he had Pixie blood on his hands? At least he'd be punished."

My stomach flip-flopped again. I wanted to talk to Jax for a moment about something, but when I opened my mouth to call for Jax, a loud horn noise sounded, sending the crowd in the stands into a fit of wild cheering. I scanned the scene to find a transparent globe in the center of the open-air room. The orb flashed green and then purple before showing a man standing in Maria's closet.

King Finvarra stood as he raised his hands. "We are now reconvening the hearing and will watch as Maxwell investigates for these so-called clues the dead human collected. Maxwell, begin your search based on the information presented in court."

The Fae in the orb nodded and held out their hands while facing the closet. A brilliant gold light filled the room, obscuring everyone's vision of the scene for a moment. When the light died down, sparkles circled around an area. Maxwell stepped forward and bent down to search the wall with his fingertips. He pushed firmly against the area where the magic concentrated, causing part of the wall to fall out. Behind the wall stood a recessed area with a book. The Courier reached into the space and retrieved the item. "My King, this is indeed a book. I will bring it to you immediately."

No sooner had the Fae spoken, he climbed out of the orb to stand before Finvarra. He kneeled and handed his recovered prize to another Fae standing next to the King. I presumed this third Fae was Lord Anders, but I wasn't for sure. The unnamed Fae examined the book by waving his hands over the cover. A blue light engulfed the book. I held my breath, waiting for someone to speak for what felt like an eternity. The Fae with the blue magic finally frowned before looking towards Finvarra. Finvarra's brow wrinkled and his cheeks flushed. Snatching the book away from the one examining the volume, Finvarra stood and chucked the book across the court. The people in the stands, previously quiet, let out a murmured gasp.

When no one moved to do anything, I walked to where Jax stood. I yanked at his shirt sleeve, breaking whatever trance he seemed to be under. "What the hell is going on, Jax? Why isn't anyone doing anything?"

Jax took my hand in his and squeezed. "The blue magic Lord Anders used is a high-level detection spell. The court only uses that kind of spell to validate unique items in high stakes cases."

"So, why did your father throw the book?"

Jax laughed. "He's angry the magic proved the book authentic."

I chewed at my lip. What good will the book do if nobody looks at the information? "Isn't he going to read the book? See what all Maria collected against Julian?"

"There's no need. The spell already summarized the contents. I assume my father is just mad to learn a human bested Julian. Most of our inhabitants here in Fairy disdain humans and see them as beneath a Fae. Sure, occasionally, a Fae gets bored and plays with a talented human for a while, but they don't keep the humans or stay in your realm; it's considered taboo."

I rolled my eyes. "This sounds like such an awesome place to live. I wonder what they think of someone like me from a mixed bloodline."

Jax pulled me closer to him in a weird side hug. "Tempy, I would like to tell you they will accept you with open arms here, but the truth is, most of the Fae will see you as tainted. They won't care how powerful you are, nor will they care you can't help your lineage."

I nodded before letting out a sigh. "Well, I guess it's a good thing I never intended to stay here in Fairy, then."

Jax's gaze fell. "My father will never let you leave Fairy."

I pulled back from Jax to look into his amber eyes. "He can't control me, Jax. If I want to go back to my life after all of this, I most certainly will. I will not stay in a place where they look down on me because of my birth."

"Tempy, it isn't that easy. Once you came back to Fairy and broke the curse, you condemned yourself to be ruled by the King. Like it or not, you are a citizen of Fairy now. As soon as we sort all this Julian mess out and Summer has a new heir, the next court will rise. Perhaps the new ruler will allow your petition to leave. In the meantime, I will shield you from the scorn of Fairy."

A sinking feeling developed in the pit of my stomach hearing Jax's words. My resolve only grew as I clenched my jaw. "I am not waiting until Summer has a new heir to leave. Don't worry Jax, I wouldn't count on me as a resident just yet."

Chapter 28

King Finvarra stood back in front of the crowd to relay his verdict. He stood up straight before speaking in an enhanced voice. "I have decided in the case of Julian Devereux, also known as King Oberon. It is with a heavy heart I must condemn our once beloved king to the Pits of Despair. He has committed a serious crime in harming our magical brethren and ignoring the rules of Fairy. Being in exile in the human world is no excuse for his atrocious actions. As a former ruler, he should know better than any other citizen our rules and regulations. His powers are to be stripped immediately, and he is to be bound in the strongest shackles before being thrown into the pit."

Finvarra snapped his fingers before a gleaming golden set of chains appeared around Julian's form. Julian pulled at the chains, but it did him no good. "Curse you! Curse all of you! I am King Oberon. You shall not throw me away like a common criminal."

Maria smirked. "You are a common criminal, Julian. A liar and a murderer. You and this pit of despair place deserve one another after everything you have caused. Happy eternity!"

Julian squirmed more under the chastising from Maria. "If you hadn't messed up all of my plans, we'd be happily married."

Maria snorted. "Thank goodness you killed me before then."

I smiled at seeing Julian looking helpless under the chains. His words had bark, but he had no bite. I walked closer to him, braver now he no longer had his magic. "Wiggle all you want, but you will never be free. Your actions will haunt you forever while the rest of us move on with our lives."

Julian's nose flared. "You think this is the end, princess? You walk into the sunset and get your happily ever after? Finvarra will use you and your powers. He will tie you to Fairy. Jax won't be able to save you from this prison!"

Before I could form a retort, Julian disappeared. His words caused me to pause. *What had I done?*

"Now, we have another matter which I must address. The channeled soul, Maria, arrived here in Fairy through unusual circumstances. Normally, I would dispatch such a being back to the ether. However, I have decided to provide restitution to her by allowing her to live a life here in Fairy. While it is unusual for a necromantic channeled soul to be allowed to remain corporeal, I believe we owe it to this entity to give her a second chance at life. If she chooses, I will use Julian's harvested magic to bring her fully into the flesh, where she will be a full Fae."

My mouth flew to my hand at the proclamation. I looked towards Maria to see her response. The wheels were turning in her mind. I held my breath, waiting for her to reply. Could I have my sister back in the flesh for all eternity?

Maria stood staring at me like a deer trapped in the beam of oncoming headlights.

A voice broke the tension. "If the lady needs a moment to decide, we can call a recess for the evening. There is no hurry."

I turned to find Anders approaching Maria with a smile as bright as his golden hair. He reached out and took her hand as if she were nothing more than another Fae. "Miss Maria, I am Lord Anders. I am a member of Fairy's High Council. I would enjoy showing you around if you decide to take his highness up on the offer to become a resident. I can see how shocked you are by the turn of today's events, but if you would like, I can convince his majesty to call for a recess, allowing you to explore all Fairy offers."

Maria blushed as a small smile cropped up on her face. "Are you sure you would want to be seen with such an abomination? You are obviously a respected member of your society. I wouldn't want to tarnish your credibility in the eyes of your people."

"My dear, you are not an abomination. You will soon find out I care little about what others think about my actions. A resident of Fairy did you a great injustice and I would like to see you compensated. If showing you around and having a meal with you helps you weigh your options, then I am more than glad to endure the glares of my brethren."

Maria floundered. I never knew my sister to be at a loss for words. Clearing my throat, I moved towards the pair. "Maria, Lord Anders here has made quite a fine suggestion. Perhaps you should see all a life in Fairy could afford you? At least take him up on his offer of a meal. No need to go back to the ether on an empty stomach, right?"

"Uhm, well, I guess." Maria fidgeted from one foot to the other.

"Princess Tempest is also welcome to join us for dinner and a tour if she likes. Seeing as she will also be a resident of Fairy."

"Oh, I will not become a resident of Fairy Lord Anders. I have parents to return to back in the human world."

Running up beside me, Jax moved to wrap his arm around my waist. "Actually, Tempest and I would love to join you and Maria for dinner. It's been a long day and I would love some huckleberry wine and rose jelly."

"Ah, splendid, Jax. I will escort Maria to my personal dwelling so she may ask questions freely. Please stop by with Tempest shortly for a meal." Anders held out his hand for Maria. "My good lady, if you will, please follow me."

Pushing Jax off me, I growled. "Why did you agree to go to dinner with him? He's obviously trying to hit on my sister. I'm sure he only extended me the offer to make Maria feel more at ease."

"Calm down, Tempy. If you want to go back to the human world, you'll need a friend like Lord Anders on the council. He can help bring your petition sooner rather than later and may force the king's hand. Besides, it's been a long day and you need to eat."

Blowing out a breath, I rolled my eyes at Jax. "Fine, we can go to dinner with Lord Anders."

"THIS MEAL WAS DELICIOUS. I don't remember having anything like it before in the human world. Of course, I didn't eat as a ghost. Death tends to reset a gal's pallet."

An amused look crossed Ander's face. "You are such an interesting person, Maria. I hope if you decide to stay, you will visit me often?"

Willing my food to stay down while watching the sickeningly sweet exchange between Anders and Maria, I jumped when something touched my hand. Looking down, I found Jax had slipped his hand into mine while by the spectacle unfolding at the dinner table kept me distracted. Leaning towards Jax, I whispered into his ear. "What the hell are you doing?"

A sly grin spread across Jax's face. "I'm holding my intended's hand at dinner."

Frustration shot through me causing me to snarl my words. "I'm not your intended, Jax. Remember, I broke the curse without having to marry anyone. There's no need to keep the pact for marriage anymore."

Jax pushed closer to me to whisper into my ear. "You can't tell me you aren't attracted to me. I know you feel the pull. Even with the curse broken, we have something. I'm not willing to turn a blind

176

eye to the feelings I have for you. Why can't you afford me the same grace?"

"I, just...I can't do this right now, Jax."

A voice pulled me back to the dinner table. "Princess Tempest, are you sure you wish to go back to the human world? We can arrange for you to have everything you need here in Fairy."

I shook my head. "I'm sorry, Lord Anders, I'm just not prepared to lead a life in Fairy. My parents think I'm on a project in New York. If I don't get home soon, they'll worry. The last daughter they let go to New York wound up dead. I can't torment them by not coming back."

Maria snorted. "Rude! It's not like I planned on being murdered."

"I know Maria! But what do you think it would do to our parents if I didn't go back to the human world? If I just disappeared to live as a princess in a magical land without so much as a goodbye? You know Mom would become institutionalized. And Dad would be all alone with nobody."

Anders sat back in his chair, folding his hands on the table in front of him. "Your devotion to your parents is commendable, Tempest. I understand the points you have made. However, returning to your home may be harder than simply wishing to do so. You are a powerful Fae and royalty here."

"Lord Anders, I came here to break a curse. I never promised to stay. That's not what I signed up for. Maria is more than welcome to choose to live here. I think she should, but I don't think Fairy is going to be hospitable to someone like myself. I am tainted, after all. Maria will become a true Fae, though, so I don't have to worry about her."

Anders ran his hands over his face before blowing out a breath. "As long as Finvarra is king, he won't let you go. As much as I love my brother, a darkness has claimed him over the years. He yearns for more and more power. At this rate, even with the curse broken, I don't think the transition will go smoothly."

Maria sighed. "Tempy, maybe it's time to tell them about what you learned from Queen Fay."

I shot a glare at my sister. I wasn't sure what I learned during my fight for the magic was real, but if Maria saw the same thing, maybe everything was true.

Anders fidgeted in his seat. "Princess Tempest, are you telling me you talked to Queen Fay?"

"During my battle for the magic, I had to fight some kind of sentient creature. At the time, I wasn't sure what was happening, but now that I know it wasn't a delusion, I think it's safe to bring forth the secrets I learned. Maybe if we worked together, Lord Anders, we could bring House Summer's reign to an end."

"I'm all ears, my dear. Please, if you can find a peaceful way for us to remove my brother from power, I will give you anything you want."

Chapter 29

I walked with my sister and Jax from Lord Anders' home to House Summer's Palace. Unlike the Summer Court from earlier, the Summer Palace was more tangible. The golden walls towered over us like great glittering giants. Dread filled my stomach, causing my grip on Jax's arm to tighten.

"Relax, Tempy. I'll be waiting for you when you come out of my father's private hall. You only need to focus on your petition and the plan, OK?"

I gulped down several huge breaths of air before nodding and allowing Jax to lead us through the entrance. Beads of sweat formed on the back of my neck. My legs betrayed me by turning into noodles, causing me to lean a little more on Jax. His arm automatically snaked around my waist, helping to support my weight. I allowed the sensation of the wind I always felt when I was close to him to wash over me and sink into my bones. I still wasn't sure how Jax always smelled so incredible, but for the moment I just went with the offered comfort.

As soon as we crossed the threshold, a Fae dressed in an opulent red and gold robe approached.

"Good evening, Jax, Tempest, and Maria. I am Rothchild, the King's personal assistant when he is at home. His majesty has been preparing for your arrival. Please follow me and I will show you to the parlor room."

The old-fashioned wording caught me off guard. "I'm sorry, did you say parlor room?"

"Yes, Lady Tempest. King Finvarra prefers to receive special guests and political meetings in his parlor room. He says the space provides for a more intimate gathering."

I felt a frown forming on my face. The selection of the venue was not at all where Anders said the King received guests. I was hoping to be in a less private area than something dubbed a parlor room.

Jax leaned over, whispering in my ear, "Don't worry about the room you meet my father in. Our plans will still work. After he helps Maria, keep him occupied and focused on you for as long as you can. Trust me."

Rothchild paused before a set of ornate doors crafted from what appeared to be solid gold. "Now, Lady Tempest and Lady Maria, if you would please enter here, the King will be with you shortly. As for you, young Jax, I need to speak to you in the library. We need to finish up the final accounting bills from your last trip to New York."

Jax huffed. "Right now, Rothchild? Are you sure this couldn't wait until next month?"

Rothchild's golden hair swayed left and right as he shook his head. "I'm afraid not, my Liege. I need to balance the books by tomorrow."

"Fine." Jax pouted, kicking at the ground like a petulant child.

Before anymore could be said, Rothchild snatched Jax down the hallway. They left Maria and me standing at the entrance, not knowing if we should knock or announce ourselves. No sooner had the thoughts left my mind, the doors opened. Standing in between the two doors was King Finvarra.

"Welcome, Maria and Tempest! Please come in and visit me for a while."

A wave of unease passed through my body at the sight of the king. Grabbing Maria's hand, we followed Finvarra through the doors and into his parlor. Unlike the open-air feeling of the communal courts, the parlor was more suffocating. The walls were dark red with heavy gold accents. Pictures of flowers and the sun hung on every wall. My chest grew heavy with a sudden thickness in the air. I hadn't had a panic attack in years, so why now?

Maria, catching my state, moved me towards a nearby couch, where we both plopped down in a most ungraceful way.

Finvarra raised a brow at us before plastering a fake smile on his face. "Well, ladies... we certainly have had an exciting day, thanks to you two. I haven't seen the nobility in such an uproar for ages. I am sure you will both keep things interesting around Fairy. Now, what brings two beautiful women to see me at such an hour? Is there something I can do for you?"

Maria, ever the diplomat, returned Finvarra's plastic smile. "Your grace, I have decided to take you up on your generous offer to allow me to become a full Fae. I've had the most wonderful tour with Lord Anders, and I believe a life here would be a just compensation for the harm Julian brought upon me by murdering me. I was so excited I dare say I wouldn't be able to sleep if I did not let you know right away."

Chuckling, Finvarra nodded his head. "Lord Anders can be very persuasive. I am most happy to see you taking me up on the offer. This act will help ease some of the negative energy Oberon put out there in the world. I know a life here in Fairy may not be a complete replacement because you can never return to the human realm, but I believe you will be happy here. Have you considered what court you'd like to be assigned to?"

"I didn't realize I could pick a court. Honestly, I know very little about the Fae world. I couldn't possibly choose without some sort of tutelage."

"Ah, then it's settled. I will assign you to House Summer, where Lord Anders can oversee your integration into our society. I am sure you will find this most agreeable, Lady Maria."

A deep red color crept across Maria's cheeks. "Uhm, yes. I would like to spend some time with Lord Anders. I feel he could teach me a great deal about my future life here in Fairy."

"Excellent! Then let it be known Lady Maria is now a Daughter of Summer. As it is spoken, as it shall be!" The king clapped his hands together before a flash of lightning flickered from them, shooting out and landing on Maria's chest.

I gasped as the little spark buried itself in her chest. With each passing second, Maria's features changed to take on a more Fae-like appearance. The most striking change was her hair. Once black as night, I watched as the strands turned a deep golden color; like the dark was being washed out as easily as dirt.

Finvarra clapped his hands once again, and an attendant appeared, holding a golden mirror. The servant presented the mirror to Maria, who reached out with a shaky hand.

"Am I so different, Tempy?"

"Maria, oh my goodness, you are spectacular! I can hardly believe you are my sister! Go on, look."

Holding the mirror up, Maria gazed at her reflection. She stared for a moment before touching her face. "This is really me? I look so much like a Fae. And look, I can see myself again!"

"You are the epitome of Fae beauty, Lady Maria. I am glad the ugliness of Oberon's magic turned you into something so beautiful. Now, not only can you lead a long life as a distinguished citizen of Fairy, but you will have the opportunity to find a suitable mate, bringing further balance from Oberon's dark deed."

Maria stood and curtsied to King Finvarra. "Thank you, your grace. I cannot wait to get my new life started here in Fairy."

"My pleasure, Lady Maria. Now, if you follow Monroe here, he will escort you to your new dwellings. I hope your home will be to your taste, but if you desire to change something, all you need to do is use your magic. I'm sure Lord Anders will be happy to assist you in magic lessons until you are used to calling forth your power."

Maria paused. "You're giving me a house? But why?"

A chuckle echoed in the chamber. "My dear, where did you think you would live? Out in a garden somewhere? You're a Fae, not a Pixie."

"No, more like a low-cost Fairy apartment, at least until I can earn enough to buy my own house."

"You have a great deal to learn about Fairy, my dear. The Courts gift all adult inhabitants with their own house upon their thirtieth birthday. And when two single Fae wed, their houses combine, quite literally, as you humans are fond of saying. You will want for nothing while you are here under my rule. I assure you; we will accord you all the privilege and perks of being a full-blooded Fae. Now, go see your new home. I will direct Lord Anders to your dwelling tomorrow afternoon to begin your training."

With a giggle, Maria followed Monroe out through the parlor doors. As soon as Maria was out of sight and the doors shut, King Finvarra sat back down across from me. "Princess Tempest, I believe we became acquainted rather negatively when you first arrived. Please, allow me to make amends to you. What would make you happy?"

Shifting in my seat under the king's gaze, I felt my stomach tap dancing. "You are most kind, your highness. You've already repaid me a great courtesy by giving Maria a new life. I no longer have to mourn her or worry about her happiness. I couldn't possibly ask you for anything more."

"Oh, come now, Tempest. You didn't trek here all the way to placate me with false pleasantries. I know there is something you want. I can see it in your eyes."

"Very well, I would like to petition His Highness, now all is well, to return to my life in the human world. I have no desire to stay here in Fairy. The only thing I want is to go back home."

"Why in the world would you want to leave, Tempest? This is your rightful home. You could claim the throne of House Autumn. Wouldn't you like to stay with your sister? I don't think she would have agreed to become a Fae if you weren't going to be here."

"I am quite certain Maria decided on her own without worrying whether I was going to be here. From what I have witnessed, I think she is going to have a lovely time getting to know Lord Anders. But the choice was simple for my sister, as she had nothing left in the human world. However, my life is waiting for me back in the human realm. My parents need me and I have a career. I can't simply fall off the face of the Earth. I've done all I can do for Maria, and she understands I need to get back. Now, the only thing I will ask for is for you to please allow me to return to the human realm as soon as possible."

Finvarra gritted his teeth. "You ungrateful mixed blood. I offered both your sister and you an elevated place here, but you refuse? In fact, you throw all my generosity back into my face! No, I will not grant your request. Get out of my sight!"

Standing from the couch, I took a step towards the king. "I would think a man with as many ghosts in his closet as you would be glad for me to return to the human world."

Slamming his hand down, Finvarra caused the glasses on the table next to him to rattle. "Empty threats and lies won't get you anything, dear. I was willing to at least marry you off to my useless son Jax, but now I'm not so sure. You seem like you may be too much trouble if left to mingle with the nobility. Perhaps an assignment in the deepest forests of Fairy looking for misguided souls would be a better use of your talents."

I looked down at Finvarra while shaking my head. I no longer cared about Fairy or punishing Finvarra for his crimes. Even with Anders' promise to me to give me anything I wanted if I brought Finvarra down, my gut told me this fight might not be worth the headache. I just wanted to go home and be done with all of Fairy.

A pain hit me in my gut as I thought back to the ravaged homeland of House Autumn. *Didn't my blood, no matter how long I've known them, deserve vengeance only I could secure?* I let out a breath I didn't realize I was holding before staring Finvarra down and recounting my tale. "At first you did everything you could to break the curse. You wanted Oberon to come back and take the throne, but after a while you came to realize having the curse persist would make you ruler indefinitely. Oberon would never come back, and your sons would never have an heir because of Kinara and Oberon's opposing curses. Endless Summer would reign here in Fairy where you never had to fear relinquishing your rule. You sacrificed Queen Fay under the guise of a plan from your advisors. You misled your people and murdered Queen Fay just to keep everyone thinking you were working tirelessly to break the curse. When, in reality, you only desired to be rid of your mate, who was becoming suspicious. The dalliance with Jax's mother was just a bonus. You never intended for Jax to be born, but you wanted to sleep with his mother. Fae may mate for life, but apparently, some of you have a wandering eye."

Red filled Finvarra's face as he shot up out of his seat. "How preposterous! You are an outsider to Fairy and know nothing about the inner workings of our system. Don't mistake your newfound powers with omnipotence, little mixed blood. You have no proof of anything you just said. I should have you executed for such baseless accusations. I loved my wife more than anything."

"I hoped you would be more reasonable, Finvarra. I have no desire to meddle in the politics of Fairy, but you leave me no choice by refusing to allow me to return home."

"We cannot allow you to return to the land of humans. I can't have a threat like you as a free agent out there. What if you decide to do something just as dastardly as Oberon? Who would stop you over in the human world? You are too powerful to remain unchecked. The safety of my citizens is at stake here. Therefore, you can never return to your home. Fairy is your home now and I am your ruler!"

I smirked. "Are you afraid I'll somehow dig up more ghosts of your past in a realm you have no authority over? One where the ghosts may not be so afraid to talk?"

Finvarra pinched the bridge of his nose. "You may be a powerful necromancer, a veil piercer, and possibly a channeler, but you can never summon ghosts from my past."

"Why? Because you sacrificed their essence to the Wheat Stone and tied them to the curse? Do you think now I broke the stone all your ghosts are gone?"

Finvarra blanched as a bead of sweat trickled down his brow. His mouth opened and closed like a fish gasping for air. I could tell he was trying to gain purchase, but came up short-handed with my revelation.

"Did you know I spoke to Queen Fay? You may have fed her to the Wheat Stone, but she guided me when I was in House Autumn's stronghold. I used my magic to make her spirit visible so her sister could see her. I didn't realize at the time, because I thought Lady finally went to rest, but she was the one who fought me during the struggle to get my magic. Only, it wasn't just my magic, was it?"

Finvarra grabbed at the hair on his head while screaming, "You couldn't possibly know any of this! Did one of my advisors turn on me?"

His slip up was just the crack I needed to dig my heels in. "So, you admit the things I have told you are true?"

"Yes! It doesn't matter though, no one will believe you. The citizens will be so overjoyed with the destruction of the curse they will choose to ignore a tainted blood like you. Even if they were stupid enough to trust you, no one would care about those tainted blood Lost Daughters I sacrificed to keep them from breaking the curse. My citizens would probably cheer knowing I was eradicating such a grievous error in our bloodline."

Something niggled at my mind, causing me to pause. "Does Jax know you used him to find those Lost Daughters to kill them?"

"Of course not. He's just a clueless boy. Every time he brought me a new candidate for breaking the curse, I sent my best operatives to leave a Changeling before he could investigate the girl further. By the time Jax went to follow up on the candidate, the Changeling was in place and turned out to be a dud. In the meantime, I brought the real tainted bloods here where I sacrificed them to the Wheat Stone to keep the curse strong. Since they didn't come here of their own free will, their mere arrival didn't weaken the curse. Not like when you barged into Fairy."

My brows squeezed together for a moment before another pain stabbed me. "How did Jax know the Changelings were duds?"

"First, he would tell the potential Lost Daughter about the curse. Most of them knew a little about Fairy from their family tales, but none of them put any clout into the stories. Once he vetted the candidate, Jax would provide us with the name and location of the girl. Last, he would take them into his little pocket dimension in Fairy at the back of his club and kiss them. If they had been the proper candidates, they might have sparked a Fae pact with him, which would be an unnecessary complication. Of course, none of them were anything more than Changelings."

Another memory nagged at me about how this situation went down between Jax and me. "Did Jax ever tell you I was a candidate?"

"No, he never mentioned you. I never heard about you until you showed up in Fairy and I felt my grip on the curse breaking."

"Hum, seems like Jax might not have been as clueless as you thought, considering he did that whole kissing pact stunt with me before I knew about my tainted blood, as you called it."

Finvarra shrugged. "The details no longer matter. Your arrival here in Fairy has caused me a great hardship. You will no longer gain any favors from me, but I will make your life here miserable."

Releasing the anger building in my body, I blew out a breath before getting into the king's face. "I wouldn't count on that, Finvarra."

"I will admit you have some audacity, but your posturing and angry words will not sway me. You could have been a princess if only you played along."

"Oh, really? I think my tenacity might surprise you." The heat in my body suddenly cooled when an autumn scented breeze washed over me causing a smile to spread across my lips. I didn't know how he got in here without being seen, but he did say to trust him. Without turning around, I called out to Jax. "Did you get all of your father's confessions on the Orb of Seeing?"

Jax stepped out from the shadows, followed by a Courier with an Orb and Lord Anders. "Yes, we caught the entire confession from Finvarra and we broadcast the whole dialogue throughout Fairy."

Finvarra turned to look at Jax, but his eyes grew wide when they landed on Anders. "You would betray me, brother? For what? I already agreed to let you have Maria. What more could you possibly want?"

"Brother, I sat here for far too long watching you destroy Fairy. Power corrupts your soul. Absolute power corrupts absolutely, remember? You and Oberon both fell prey to your love of control. But look where that love affair has gotten you. Tempest's story confirmed what I suspected all along. Fay didn't deserve to die because of your lust. At least part of your prophecy came true. A child of winter and a child of summer helped break the curse. Take

Finvarra away! The High Council will strip him of his powers immediately. Final sentencing will be in a week's time."

Two armed Fae rushed in to shackle a screaming Finvarra. Once the king had been removed, Anders turned off the Orb of Seeing ending the transmission. As soon as the room fell quiet, I felt the tightness in my chest release. "So, now what? Who will run House Summer without Finvarra? I still need someone to hear my petition."

Jax smiled at me half-heartedly. "Don't worry Tempest, Lord Anders has the authority to take charge of House Summer since they arrested Finvarra."

Turning, I smiled at Anders. "Good. I think House Summer could use a change in leadership. Now, will Lord Anders hear my petition?"

"I most certainly will, Lady Tempest."

Chapter 30

"If everyone could please allow Lady Tempest and I a moment of respite to discuss her petition. I will brief the council and the other heads of the houses tomorrow morning. For now, I'd like everyone to get some rest. We have a lot of work to do."

I stood watching all the onlookers file out of the parlor room. When Jax started to leave, I grabbed his hand. "Shouldn't you stay here with us? You are as much a part of this plan as I am."

Jax pulled his hand out of mine, taking a step back. "Hey, don't worry, Tempy. You've got this. I'm sure Lord Anders will give you what you want. Look, I have to go. I'm not a recognized member of royalty here. I'll see you later."

Before I could say anything more, Jax disappeared through the double doors before they slammed shut. It was now my turn to stand around like a fish gasping for air.

"Tempest, you don't have to worry about this meeting. I'm not here to deny your petition or rake you over the coals. I merely wanted to ask if you would help me with some things before you leave."

I spun around, directing my attention to Anders. "What can I possibly help you with? I'm not exactly going to be Miss Popularity around here."

"While it is true the nobles may have no love for your tainted blood, the common Fae have taken a shine to you. The broadcast numbers show you are a popular lady. That's why, before I help you back to your old life, I need you to set the citizens of Fairy straight.

They seem to think you are going to ascend the throne and rule Fairy."

"What? I don't know the first thing about ruling a magical realm."

"I figured you would say something along those lines. That's why I was hoping you'd give a public broadcast and let everyone know of your plans before you left."

"Uhm, sure. I can make an announcement if you think it would help smooth things over when everyone finds out I'm not staying."

"There's one other thing I want you to do. Could you talk to Jax and convince him to accept his mother's proposal to have a place in House Winter? With House Summer in chaos and House Autumn down an heir and a ruler, the next viable court would be House Winter. However, that's only if Jax accepts his place as the heir."

"Shouldn't that be up to Jax? Why would you want me to convince him to take a job I know nothing about? From what I understand, both courts have treated Jax rather poorly. His mother abandoned him for a throne and his father used him as a pawn. And you want me to convince him to stay here and be in line to rule?"

"Yes. If he were to accept the position, it would make this transition more palatable to the nobles, and the job would keep Jax's mind focused."

"Why would he need his mind to be focused on something so exhausting as ruling?"

"Because you're leaving him, Tempest. My nephew has had a rough time of it here. I won't deny what I know you've seen. But he has never looked at anyone the way he looks at you. Tempest, I think he loves you and when you go back, it's going to destroy him because he won't have anything to occupy his time anymore. I think if you convince him to rule, he'll take the job."

"Look, I will do what I can to help you, but Jax isn't in love with me. If he feels anything, it's residuals from the curse. That's what was pushing us together. Plus, I think we are in some kind of marriage pact. If Jax would dissolve the pact and let me leave, I'm sure his feelings would disappear."

Anders' expression on his face fell slack. "Right, well, could you at least try to get him to accept the invitation? His mother never abandoned him. Finvarra tried to keep Morganna away from Jax. Finvarra ordered her to take the throne of House Winter and leave House Summer forever. She didn't have a choice. My brother only wanted to use her and throw her away."

Rubbing my face, I nodded. "Alright, I'll try to convince Jax to visit House Winter and let him know about his mother's plight. I can't make any promises he will become the heir, but I will try to get him on board with the idea."

"Great, for now I want you to rest. I've assigned you a room in the east wing of the palace. Seeing as you are leaving, I didn't think you would need a house like Maria."

A yawn escaped my lips at the word rest while my eyelids drooped. "Oh, yes, rest would be great. I feel like I could sleep for a week. I'm sure it's way past my normal bedtime, anyway."

I CLIMBED WHAT FELT like a million stairs to get to the room Lord Anders directed me towards. When my hand finally landed on the double doorknob of my assigned room, a voice in the hallway deflated my hopes of sleep.

"Tempy, can we talk?"

I flung the doors open and gestured for Jax to follow me into the room. I didn't care if it was proper or not. I was tired, and I wanted to sleep, but I also needed to talk to Jax about his mother. "Fine, but if I fall asleep, just poke me, OK?"

A wicked grin flashed over Jax's face. "I'd like to poke you, but I'd rather you were awake when I did."

"Jax, what are you in middle school? Can you focus with your brain and not what's in your pants? I swear, are males all the same in every realm?"

Jax laughed before pulling me into his arms. "Tempy, I don't want you to leave Fairy. Now that I have completed all my tasks in the human world, I don't know when or if I will return. This whole curse thing has caused such a ruckus. I'm sure there's going to be a ban on travel for most Fae folks. I'll be incredibly bored here without something to do. At least in the human world, I had crimes to solve and bad guys to catch."

"Well, Jax, I might have something to occupy your time here in Fairy, regardless of if I return home or not."

Jax pulled back enough for me to look up into his eyes. He cocked his brow up. "Like what?"

"I don't know how to explain this, so I'm going to spit it out. Your father kept your mother away from you. He ordered her to accept the throne in House Winter after you were born. Now your father is no longer an obstacle. Morganna has reached out to Lord Anders to offer you an official position as the heir to House Winter."

Jax rolled his eyes. "After all these years, you expect me to believe my mom wants something to do with me? And you want me to become a prince?"

"Jax, I can't pretend I understand these weird politics of the houses, but Summer and Autumn are in no shape to rule right now. So, the best thing to do is to have House Winter step up. They are next in the rotation after House Autumn. Your uncle believes it would be more palatable an idea if House Winter presented with an heir before the takeover. You taking the role would help solidify your mother's claim to rule, especially since as long as Finvarra lives she's unable to claim a new mate."

"Why can't you become the leader of House Autumn? The citizens of Fairy adore you already. They wouldn't care if you had an heir."

"You know I can't stay here. My parents wouldn't recover from losing me and Maria. I know you don't understand having a bond with your parents, but surely you can understand that simply disappearing on someone without a trace is not a good idea?"

"I think I can, but Tempy, I won't be able to see you if you leave. And becoming an heir would keep me busy for hours on end."

"If you took the heir position, couldn't you bend the rules? Maybe in time you could come see me in the human world? If your mother is in charge and things settle down, maybe everything will get better."

Jax frowned as his amber eyes flashed red. "Did my uncle condition your petition to return home on my accepting the heir position?"

"No, I only told your uncle I would talk to you about the possibility. He thought you might consider the proposal coming from me. I have to make an announcement to renounce my throne and I'd like to announce your acceptance of the heir position before I leave. I just think in the grand scheme of things you becoming an heir and me leaving Fairy would allow everything to settle down."

Jax stepped back away from me throwing his head back. "If this is what you truly desire, I'll accept the heir position. I'll find some way to see you again. Maybe you're right about being able to bend the rules if I'm a Prince of House Winter. Hopefully, my agreement will secure your ability to return home to your parents."

I couldn't stand the hurt look on Jax's face. Wrapping my arms around him, I laid my head on Jax's chest inhaling his cool autumn wind scent, most likely for the last time. I may not miss Fairy when I leave, but I would miss this comforting smell. As my body relaxed in Jax's arms, my eyes grew tired of waiting for sleep and snapped closed.

The last thing I remember before falling into the void of sleep was being tucked into bed and cocooned in warm arms.

Chapter 31

"Alright, Tempest, I've prepared the transmission orb. Are you ready to speak to all of Fairy?"

Blowing out my breath, I nodded. "Yup, this will be exactly like giving one of my interviews back home. Just let me know when you're ready for me to speak."

Unlike the Orb of Seeing, this sphere was much larger. Jax explained to me the larger the orb, the further the transmission can reach. The blue orb we stood in front of now was at least six feet in diameter and used to reach every corner of Fairy. Lord Anders nodded and turned to face the device before signaling to an attendant. The attendant waved his hands like a conductor beginning the process. The orb glowed a bright white before spinning and floating above its cradle. A humming noise filled the room, and then a soft tone dinged. I could only assume this meant the orb was transmitting to Fairy because Lord Anders began his address.

"Citizens of Fairy, as many of you have heard by now, we have removed King Finvarra from his position. We found evidence condemning the king late last night after the trial of Oberon. Currently, since House Summer is still technically the ruling class, I have taken over the throne per our house protocol during an arrest of a ruling king. A full report of Finvarra's crimes and the evidence against him will be available for review for any interested citizen by the end of this week. The next order of business is putting several rumors to rest once and for all. For this, I turn to Princess Tempest of House Autumn."

Nodding, I moved forward to speak into the center of the transmission device. I gave a slight smile before launching into my pre-rehearsed statement. "Greetings citizens of Fairy. My name is Tempest Danvers, and I am a Lost Daughter from House Autumn. I am a direct descendant of Kinara and, until recently, I was a resident of the human realm. I am here today to address several rumors which have surfaced in the few hours since I've made myself known to Fairy. Contrary to what some report, I am not here to take over House Autumn or overthrow your government. Bringing to light the wrongs of King Finvarra was something only I could do because of my unique magic and relation to the original curse. My bloodline had a hand in starting this curse, and now my bloodline has had a hand in ending the curse which has held you all captive for so many years. I will admit, though, the rumors about me advising the interim ruler of House Summer about how Fairy should proceed are true. My breaking of the curse, refusal to accept the crown of House Autumn, and my hand in overthrowing your Summer King have all caused a true power conundrum. Both House Summer and House Autumn need time to recover from years of being cursed, as neither is fit to rule over Fairy at this time. However, House Winter not only has a ruler but also an heir—Prince Jax. Although completely unconventional, allowing House Winter to rise and rule would afford House Summer and House Autumn breathing room to put their affairs in order. I know traditions are comforting and dependable, but this is a new era here in Fairy and as such, the inhabitants of Fairy must adapt. Rest assured; The High Council has not made these decisions in haste. In time, the new will once again return to your expected traditions."

Once I finished my speech, I concluded by nodding to Lord Anders. He said a few more words, then signaled for the attendant to cut the transmission. The orb grew dark and floated back down into the cradle.

Lord Anders smiled at me. "You did well for someone who has no desire to rule. Are you sure you wouldn't reconsider taking up the lead for House Autumn?"

"I assure you, Anders, I have no desire to rule anything other than my own life. I only hope I was convincing enough to put down any rumors surrounding the events from the past few days. I may not want to rule, but I want to make sure I don't leave Fairy in rampant chaos. I am leaving my favorite sister here to live, after all."

Anders folded his hands behind his back. His gaze lowered to the ground as his brows knitted together. "You're definitely leaving, then?"

I sucked my bottom lip in over my teeth while looking up at the ceiling. I couldn't look Anders in the eye any more than he could look me in the eye. "Yes, I need to get back to the human world. It's better for everyone if I leave. I know Maria will be happy here."

"Maria will have a happy life here and will want for nothing. But I'm not worried about your sister adapting to Fae life. I'm worried about what Jax will do."

"What Jax does from here on out is up to Jax. He's no longer his father's pawn. He told me if he accepted the heir position, he would have plenty to keep himself busy with. Jax needs to learn the ins and outs of being an heir and bond with his mother; we both know he won't do either of those things if I'm around."

Anders nodded. "Are you at least going to tell him goodbye before you leave?"

"I haven't decided. I'm on my way over to Maria's house to see how she has settled into her new life."

"Very well. Please let Lady Maria know if I can be of service to her with anything she only needs to ask."

I laughed at his offer. It was painfully obvious he was smitten with my newly made Fae sister. Maybe that's why I wasn't sad leaving her behind in this world she was never supposed to be a part of, because I knew Anders would take care of her. "I'll let her know, but you must promise me one thing above all. I see the way you look at her and I'm sure she's just as interested as you. But I need to make sure you understand I can't have you breaking Maria's heart. I may leave Fairy behind, but that doesn't mean I won't be getting one of those communication crystals where I can call her. If I catch one whiff of you hurting her after all she has been through, I will come back here and kick your ass with my ancestral magic. Are we clear, Lord Anders?"

"My dear, I would do nothing to bring forth your wrath. You need not worry about Maria or Jax. I will see to their wellbeing and happiness as long as I shall live."

"Awesome. Then I'll be on my way. I hope to see you before I leave."

Turning, I walked out of the transmission room, making my way to my sister's new house. Oddly, I didn't need a map or anything. I only had to follow a feeling of where the house was. It wasn't a surprise to find her new residence was suspiciously close to Lord Anders' home. I guess being close in proximity would make the inevitable merging of the homes easier.

I reached the door of Maria's dwelling, which flew open before I even knocked. On the other side, a very hyper Fae Maria jumped up and down.

"Tempy! This house is fantastic. Did you know the kitchen cooks food on its own and I can change the layout of the floor plan by just waving my hand? I thought our apartment house was awesome, but this is a designer's dream. Oh my gosh, these would be so fun to design and sell. Too bad humans don't have magic."

Walking through the door, I stop for a moment because the layout currently in front of me was the floor plan to the apartment house Maria and I shared back in Kentucky. Tears pricked the corners of my eyes. "You made your new house look like our home."

"Yeah, I thought you might be more comfortable over here if the surroundings were familiar. Do you like it?"

"Oh, Maria, this interior is a sight for sore eyes! Are you certain you want to stay here in Fairy? I'm sure I could find some way to get you back to the human world. You could come with me."

"Tempy, what do I have left to return to in the human world? I can't design clothes. I wouldn't ever be able to be seen by anyone who knows I died. Could you imagine the level of shock seeing me alive would give to anyone who saw me, even if I could convince people I wasn't me? I mean, sure, I could use some kind of glamour, but do you honestly think Mom and Dad wouldn't know me even if I looked different? Besides, I feel like I could do a lot with this magic in this land. I might start a design revolution. Maybe I can make the latest Fae fashions? At least now we'll live a long time together, right? So, maybe in a few hundred years we can revisit me coming back. But for now, I think I should stay here."

A smirk crossed my lips. "Are you sure you aren't being swayed somewhat by a certain new neighbor?"

Maria's face flushed. "Well, it certainly doesn't hurt to have good neighbors, but Leif is only helping me to adjust here. There's nothing going on between us."

"Leif? His name isn't Anders?"

"No, silly. What kind of first name would Anders be?"

I shrugged. "I don't know. What kind of Fae house name is Anders?"

"Apparently, adult Fae are free to change their names. Many of them don't have a last name unless they need one for something in the human realm. Leif used to be a liaison in the human world, so he needed a last name. The name stuck, and he became Lord Anders instead of Lord Leif."

"Right, well, I threatened your new neighbor earlier and told him I will come back and kick his magical ass if he hurts you. You're allowed to be happy, Maria, and if he makes you happy, I say go for it."

Maria crossed her arms over her chest before cocking her head. "Says the girl who's leaving the only guy I've ever seen her drool over to go back to a boring life."

"A magical curse tainting our emotions isn't the same thing as what you and Anders are feeling. Even if Jax had actual non-curse manifested feelings for me, I'm not sure what to do. I don't want to stay here in Fairy and he's royalty now. Plus, I can't just abandon Mom and Dad. I don't think Dad would survive both of us being gone. That leaves me with only one hand to play, which is going back to being Tempest Danvers, boring human."

"Do you honestly believe you'd be stuck in Fairy if you admit you have feelings for Jax?"

"Let's call it my intuition. Now that Jax is being recognized as a royal in his mother's court, I think he likes it here. I can't imagine he'd want to split his time between the human world and Fairy. It'd be selfish to demand that level of commitment from him now that he finally has his birthright."

"OK. I will not argue with you anymore about your decision. We have years to figure our futures out. We'll keep in touch with one of those communication orbs and who knows, maybe in ten years you'll come back to stay. Anyway, when do you leave?"

"That's part of the reason I came over today. I wanted to see you one last time. I don't want anyone to know I've left until they realize I've already gone back home."

Maria drummed her fingers on her arms. "Especially Jax, right?"

I shook my head before reaching behind my neck to unfasten the clasp to my sister's pea pod necklace. Taking her hand, I dropped the pendant and chain into her palm. "Yeah. I just want to walk out of here with no entanglements or regrets. I have to go back to the human world. Like you said, maybe in ten years I can come back, but for now, I've gotta go. I wish you and Leif a happy ending. Be sure to call me when you can, especially after I end up with a bunch of nieces and nephews, OK? I love you, Maria. I'm happy we could solve your murder. Good luck in your new life."

Bolting out my sister's house, I ran back towards the palace. Even though I knew I was doing the right thing by going back home, the ache in my chest seemed to disagree. Maybe one day I could return and live a life here with Maria. I would hold on to that hope, but for now, I needed to get back to my home in Kentucky ASAP.

By the time I reached the door to my room, I had already decided I was leaving Fairy in the next few minutes. Lucky for me, Anders showed me how to create a portal back home on my own earlier in the day. I think he believed I was going to dine and dash when he taught me the technique. Maybe the lesson was his way of giving me an open-ended choice. With the ability to create a portal, I could choose when I left without anyone's permission or help.

Even though I knew Anders wouldn't agree with my choice to leave without a goodbye, I didn't want to look Jax in the eye and walk away. Having to leave Jax would be hard. Truth be told, I had grown fond of him, but when you are an adult, you can't simply abandon all your responsibilities for a relationship that was probably built on false feelings. Hopefully, in time, Jax will take a bride, fulfill his obligations as an heir, and forget about me. Even though the inhabitants of Fairy might accept Jax, I knew deep down they would never accept me because of my mixed blood. There was no way I was going to ruin Jax's chance at being king one day by tying him to me.

Cracking open the door, I slipped inside my assigned room, careful not to make too much noise. Once inside, I began gathering what few possessions I had. As I stuffed items into a bag haphazardly, a package on the desk caught my eye. Walking over to investigate what was in the box, I was happy to see a small communication orb. Pulling the orb out of the container, I spun it around in my hand before stuffing the orb into my pocket. I would have time to look at the device later, after I was safely at home. A voice from behind startled me.

"Anders sent me here to help you learn how to use the orb."

Turning around, I found Jax standing behind me. *Damn Anders!* I bet he did this on purpose, so I couldn't simply disappear. He wanted me to tell Jax goodbye. Patting my pocket, I smiled. "I'm sure I'll figure this out later. Right now, I need to focus on packing."

Without warning, Jax stepped closer to tower over me. "Were you going to leave Fairy without so much as a goodbye?"

"Don't be such a drama queen, Jax. You and I both knew I was going to have to leave Fairy. The extra time I told my parents I needed to follow up on a hot lead for my new book is almost up. I can't be late getting back home."

"So that's it? You're going to get me to agree to be the heir and then ditch me?"

"No, Jax, it's not like that and you know it. I was hoping if I slipped out, there wouldn't be a chance for any awkward discussions about our futures. You know, like we're having right now."

"Tempy, I know you think I'm crazy, but even with all the curses broken, I still have feelings for you. I realize at the time of making the Fae pact with you, you didn't understand, but you agreed to marry me. All of this may be on the non-traditional side, but now I'm asking you for real. Tempest Danvers, will you marry me?"

Letting out a quick grunt, I shook my head. "So, you want me to marry you on some technicality? This Fae pact is clearly clouding your judgement. I don't want to marry someone for my entire life based on a curse or pact. I want to fall in love with someone and get married. No weird magic involved. No family curses. No crazy legacies. Look, I'm sorry, Jax, but I don't think your feelings about us are genuine. Besides, we've already discussed I can't stay here. I need to get back to my family. I can't put them through losing another daughter."

"But a Fae pact is binding. We must honor the pledge. Please reconsider leaving. I'll find some way for you to get back to your parents so you can tell them you're moving. I'll even rent an entire apartment for you to have a convincing address. I just don't think I can do this heir thing without you. I need you by my side."

"Look, Jax, you said it yourself; I didn't know what the pact was. Unlike when I entered one with Julian, I did not know such a thing existed when I met you. And since I didn't know what the pact was, you can dissolve the agreement because under Fae law it's not binding if one party is clueless. We broke the curse on Fairy and you're a noble in the Winter Court. Plus, your mother wants a relationship with you. You've held a grudge against her for far too long. Now we know why she stayed away. I think your family is what you should focus on. Not chasing some cursed tainted blood girl you only think you love."

Jax's jaw clenched as he bit down on his teeth before storming out of my room. Sighing, I figured it was now or never. Holding up my hand, I chanted the way Anders taught me to open the portal. The magic glowed with a bright purple light before an opening materialized in front of me, allowing me to step back into Loft 36.

Chapter 32: 6 Months Later

I took a deep breath while shaking out my hands. Butterflies cannonballed in my stomach while waiting for Carmilla's signal to start the interview. She smiled at me right before she twirled her finger in a little circle indicating we were live. I sat up straight and looked into the camera of my laptop while plastering a huge, fake smile on my face. I prayed my new pink hair didn't look too garish on the live feed.

"Today, we are happy to welcome back one of our favorite authors, Tempest Danvers! Everyone, please give Miss Danvers a round of applause for taking time out of her busy writing schedule to speak to us." Carmilla smiled as the cameras panned around the wildly clapping audience.

Once the clapping died down, Carmilla looked towards the camera. "Miss Danvers, thank you for coming back to my show. I'm excited about this recent novel you've written. Can you tell us more about *Silenced by Suicide: Murder in Loft 36—A Tempest Danvers Supernatural Tale*?"

"Thank you Carmilla. I'm so happy to speak with you all today about my new book. *Loft 36*, for short, deviates from my normal stories. Instead of my usual hard boiled murder mystery, I moved towards a more magical setting."

Carmilla's eyes lit up. "I noticed this novel is different because it reads a lot like a fantasy. Can you tell us why you left your tried-and-true formula for this new twist?"

"I felt it was time to spice things up in my novels. I love my fans and I love all my previous books, but sometimes inspiration strikes, and you just have to hold on and enjoy the ride. I worked non-stop on this book because I couldn't stop writing. I had all these ideas flying about in my head and I ran with them."

Carmilla raised a brow before flashing me a crooked smile. "By spicing things up, do you mean the new romantic sub-plots in this book?"

I felt my cheeks heat before letting out my smile. "I will admit romantic plots aren't usually my normal fare, but the relationship with Maxwell Devereaux kind of crept into the story. I wasn't even aware of the tale I was weaving until it was too late. One minute it's all murder mystery and then the next I have magic and this relationship. All I can say is I think this book is some of my best work."

Carmilla smiled as she fanned herself with her note cards. "Well, I can tell you feedback from our early reader groups has been overwhelmingly positive and they most definitely are loving Maxwell. I think you've hit the nail on the head with this character!"

"I am glad the early readers are excited. I hope by this time next week I'll have enchanted many more readers."

"There is no doubt in my mind you'll do just that. I've heard this book is your most pre-ordered novel, if that tells us anything. But fans are curious why the new heroine in the book is named Tempest Danvers. Is this going to be a new series featuring a character based on you?"

I laughed while shaking my head. "No, I never meant to keep the main character named after me. You see, when I write quick drafts, I often name a character after someone I know as a placeholder. It helps me keep up my momentum. I was in such a hurry to get this draft to my agent I forgot to replace all the character names. In my next round of edits, I went back and change the names, but my editor thought it would be fun to keep this character in the book named after me because she's an author. I can assure you, Tempy is nothing like me."

"So, you aren't telling the world you are a Fae princess married to a hot Fae cop prince?"

I hated the twinkle in Carmilla's eyes at the question. The query punched me harder than I thought, even though I knew it was all in fun. I winked and giggled. "One could only wish to be a royal from Fairy and marry a guy like Maxwell. Unfortunately, Fairy and Maxwell are as made up as all my other characters."

The music to notify us of the break for set change played while I sat there with a fake smile plastered on my face, willing myself not to sob.

Carmilla faced her audience, blasting them with her dazzling host smile. "Thank you once again for coming onto the show, Tempest! Everyone, please be sure to check out Tempest's new book, which drops on February 29th!"

A tightness pulled in my chest as I waited for the all-clear notice. I didn't know if I was going to make it to the signal before I lost my cool. I tried taking a few deep breaths to calm my quivering gut. Beads of sweat formed on my brow. Finally, the show cut my live feed and went to commercial. Normally I would hang around and talk to Carmilla, but I was about to lose my cool. I opened the chat box feature in the software and typed out a quick note to Carmilla letting her know I had to go and couldn't stay to chat because of another last-minute appointment. I didn't wait for her to reply before slamming the top of my laptop closed, cutting off the connection.

Tears burst out from my eyes as I tried to surf the waves of nausea assaulting me. Since coming back from Fairy, I had picked up the pieces of my human life. With my sister's murderer punished and her now having a second chance at a life, no matter how weird the situation seemed, I didn't have any regrets coming back to an ordinary world, not even leaving Maria in Fairy.

In fact, writing the fantastic adventure featured in *Loft 36* kept me sane and allowed me to put that chapter of my life behind me. The only thing that really bothered me was the stupid romance I had subconsciously woven into the story. A magical murder mystery with a twist of romance! My publishing house loved the idea so much there was no way I could revise the manuscript to take out Maxwell Devereaux or the happily ever after my brain penned for him and Tempest. The whole scenario was ludicrous, but the beta readers couldn't get enough.

Taking a few more deep breaths, I finally stood up from my office chair and made my way to my bed. I planned on cocooning myself deep into my blankets. I prayed my nap would be ghost free, but since accepting my Fae powers, I didn't have many dreamless sleeps. At least the restless ghosts haunting me kept me supplied with infinite story ideas. I peeled back the three comforters on my bed before diving in under them. I used the sleeve of my shirt to wipe away the rogue tears running down my cheek. My eyes closed, and I let go, falling into oblivion.

I slept for what felt like forever before a pounding startled me awake. I struggled to figure out what kind of weird noise I was hearing. I rolled over to see my alarm clock. I squinted at the numbers, confused because the clock read midnight. The pounding continued before I realized someone was at my door. Did somebody think I was going to come to the door in the middle of the night? I reached for my cell phone, flicking open my security system app. I checked to make sure I set the alarms and all the doors remained locked. Satisfied the house was secure, I flipped open my doorbell camera app. The feed showed a tall male pounding on my front door. I frowned when I realized he was too tall for the camera to pick up his face. The stranger paced down my small porch, grabbing at his hair before returning to my door to pound some more. This time I saw his face in the camera and I realized he was no stranger.

Agitation ran through me as I pressed the talk button on my camera. "What the hell do you want? It's midnight and I'm trying to sleep."

"Tempest! Are you seriously going to leave me out here pounding on your door in the middle of the night? I know you spent a lot of time in New York, but what about good old southern hospitality?"

"You forget, I'm not from the south. Besides, proper decorum requires you to make an announced visit for hospitality."

"Can't you give me five minutes to talk? I tried to give you enough time to adjust, but damn Tempy, it's been six months."

I scrubbed my hands over my face. I didn't want to see Jax, but I knew if I didn't hear him out, he would only come back again and again. I just wanted to be done with Fairy, but Fairy apparently wasn't done with me. I swung my legs off the bed and shoved my feet into my house shoes. I begrudgingly walked out of my bedroom and to the front door. The scent of leaves and fall wind hit my nose before I even pulled open the door. I sucked in a breath as my traitorous heart leaped at the sight of Jax and his stupid amber eyes. I motioned for him to come into the house. As I pointed to the small couch in the front room, I kept my mouth shut.

Jax nodded and made his way over to the sofa. He crashed down before looking up and flashing me a killer smile. In the past, I melted whenever he smiled at me, but now the expression only irritated me. I walked over to him and stood with my arms crossed. "OK, now tell me why you are pounding on my door in the middle of the night?"

"I wanted to see you. I've missed you. Tempy, I know you don't believe me, but I haven't stopped thinking about you."

I rolled my eyes. "We've been through this, Jax. The curse led you to me, and your stupid Fae pact is apparently interfering with your ability to resolve those created feelings. You're not actually in love with me. Besides, there is no future for us, even if you were. I live here and you wanted to stay in Fairy."

Jax sat back and crossed his legs before throwing his head back to look at the ceiling. "Can you honestly tell me you haven't missed me? Thought about me? You've been able to put all of Fairy behind you with no regrets?"

"Yes, Jax, I have moved on. I closed that chapter of my life. Maria is happy, and I brought her killer to justice. I broke all the curses, removed a corrupt tyrant, and made sure they recognized you as royalty in Fairy. Everyone should be happy now. If you'd simply dissolve the Fae pact, I think you'd be able to move on like me."

Raising an eyebrow, Jax frowned at me. "Do you expect me to believe that hogwash story, Tempy? You're a better caliber writer. You need to do better with your reasoning."

"It's not a story, Jax! Damn it, why can't you get it through your head? I'm not in love with you!"

Jax jumped up from the couch, closing the distance between us. Before I could move, he pulled me into his arms. "Tempest Danvers, I want to be with you for all eternity. Where you go, I will go. I only wish to worship at your altar from this day forward. Even if a curse started my love for you, there's no denying what I feel for you is real."

Tears pricked at my eyes. "Quoting my novel to me won't get me to change my mind. I made the entire story up, Jax."

"You expect me to believe your heart didn't pen those words? You want me to think you didn't secretly wish I had fought harder to keep you from leaving Fairy? Come on, Tempy. I proposed to you, and I didn't even get so much as a goodbye? No one would tell me where you were going after I found out that you left. I looked for you for weeks. You're getting good at covering your tracks, but I knew you'd eventually come back here."

I buried my face in Jax's chest, breathing deeply, while he rubbed his hands up my back. "How long have you been stalking me, then?"

"I didn't have to. When I heard about your book release, I knew you'd be here. Right where I found you when we started this journey."

"This doesn't change anything, Jax. I don't want to be with someone who only loves me because they're bewitched. Look, I'm glad you helped me catch Maria's killer, and that I could break a few curses gone wild, but the adventure is over. You can go back to Fairy and find a nice Fae girl to settle down with." I pushed out of his arms and moved towards the front door. Opening it, I pointed for Jax to leave.

Jax threw up his hands. "Fine, I'll go. I really hoped things would be different this time. By the way, I dissolved our contract months ago. When I came back and found you'd left, I ended the pact right then. I hoped once I ended the agreement, you'd realize the truth, but you're still rejecting me even after all this time. Since you believed everything was magic, I wanted to see if your feelings had changed. I guess I was wrong about the situation. Have a pleasant life, Miss Danvers."

Jax's words punched a hole in my gut. If he dissolved the pact months ago, then why did he still think he loved me? Before I could take another breath, Jax vanished. Slamming the door closed, I let the anguish roll through me as I slid against the door in a deluge of tears. It's times like these I hated not having Maria by my side.

Chapter 33

An unrelenting wave of sadness washed over me before I could stop crying. Leaning back on the door, I allowed myself to slide down to the floor. The weight of what I said to Jax hit me like a ton of bricks. *If I didn't have any feelings for him, why am I crying? Why did him walking out hurt so damned bad?*

"Oh Tempy, my dear sweet girl. This is exactly why I told you not to get involved with Jax. Fae men always end up making us cry. That's part of the reason Kinara escaped to the human world."

"Trust me, human men can make women cry just as much. It's part of the reason I've not pursued any actual relationships. I found not letting men in general get close to you is a sure-fire way to keep a heart from breaking."

"Are you sure the pact, the curse, and the fear of Jax realizing he doesn't love you for real are the actual reasons you keep pushing him away?"

Snot ran down my face and I absentmindedly wiped at the goo with my sleeve. *There goes that designer shirt.* "What do you mean?"

"I may not have been here in the flesh, but Tempy, I know you've done nothing but take care of everyone but yourself for your whole life. Your mom, your sister, your stepdad, and, to an extent, even the ghosts you write about in your books. But not once have I seen you truly follow what you want."

"That's not true! I have a glorious life here and I get to write these crazy stories. I'm doing everything I ever wanted to do."

"Is that true? Or are you afraid allowing yourself to even hope to be with Jax would take you away from your life here, so you don't even entertain your own feelings? Because you can't stand the thought of abandoning your parents, especially your mom?"

"I don't have feelings for Jax."

"The story you wrote would lead me to believe otherwise."

"Not you too, Gamma! How did you even read the story, anyway? You're a ghost and I'm pretty sure there isn't a library in the great beyond."

Gamma's nose crinkled as she smirked. "I watched you write your book, silly. I may not have a library card, but I can read over your shoulder."

Groaning I thumped my head onto my front door. "Even if it were true, Gamma, I think I've burned the ship before it even left port."

"Alright, let's say the Jax ship has sunk. If you could do anything without fear of what anyone would say, what would you do? Where would you go?"

I sighed. I knew the answer deep in my bones. The moment I got back to Kentucky, I knew. "I miss New York. I want to go back and visit or even move there. Being there again made me happy. Kentucky is fine and all, but I never wanted to leave New York. I had to because I was a kid, but something about the place resonates in my bones."

"I understand perfectly, Tempy. New York is a beacon to the Fae outside of Fairy. Those who must work in the human realm prefer to be around New York. The good news though, I'm pretty sure your parents wouldn't object to you going on a vacation or even moving. Your mom isn't a fragile soul anymore, Tempy. But I don't have to point all of this out, do I?"

"No, you're right. Mom has been good for a long time. I just don't know how I would explain wanting to go back so soon, though."

"That's the beauty of it all, Tempy. You're an adult. You don't have to convince anyone but yourself. It's time for you to stand on your own two feet and choose a path you want."

Chapter 34: 9 Months Later

Tired of looking at potential living spaces, and hearing Jane drone on and on about each place, I drug myself back to my hotel. I wanted nothing more than to sink my body into the huge jacuzzi tub in my suite. Thinking about the amenities waiting for me back in my room brought a smile to my lips. After today's events, having a place full of luxury to pamper myself with sounded wonderful. I was suddenly glad I splurged on this vacation and opted for one of the plusher hotels. Heck, Mom even encouraged upgrading my package at the resort and to look for property I loved instead of settling on something cheap. I had plenty of money and the rest of my life to enjoy. For once, I felt as if the sky was the limit. Unfortunately, my feet argued otherwise. One of these days, I'd find those boots that were made for walking. Until then, I had blistered feet to soak.

Walking through the suite door, I threw my keycard on the table and kicked off my shoes. Turning on some relaxing music to play through the room's audio network, I headed straight for my date with the fancy tub of my dreams.

Content with the comforting chords of *Moonlight Sonata* filling the air, I flipped the switch to heat the marble floors before running the hot water into the tub. Not one to miss a chance at more indulgence, I grabbed the bottle of rose bubble bath and threw some into the water. Did bubble bath and jacuzzi tubs go together? I didn't know, and I didn't care. No sooner had I turned off the water and undressed a horrible thumping noise assaulted my ears. The bass pulsed so hard I felt it in my head.

Annoyed, I marched out of the bathroom and grabbed the room phone. I punched 0 to reach the front desk.

A chirpy voice answered. "Front desk, how may I help you?"

"Hello, I'm in suite 500 and for some reason, it sounds as if there is a nightclub above my head. What in the world is going on?"

"I'm so sorry, miss. The noise is coming from the penthouse suite. We have tried numerous times to remind the occupants of our noise policy, but we have had little luck. The police are remiss to come for such a trivial manner with any urgency, and the occupants refuse to leave."

"Are you serious? So, what I just have to be annoyed? I'm tired and I want to relax, but I can't because some douche bag is upstairs having a hissy and you can't get them to leave?"

"We're very sorry, miss. We are doing everything we can. I will be glad to comp you on your stay to make up for the annoyance."

I rolled my eyes. "Unbelievable. Sure, you go ahead and do that, but in the meantime, I'm going to look for a different hotel. I'll be sure to let my publishing agency to not book me here again." I slammed down the receiver before I heard the lady's response. It wasn't her fault, per se, but still. *What kind of ass hat acts like this in a hotel?*

Gritting my teeth, I decided to check out this nuisance myself. If they were going to ruin my evening, I was going to barge in on theirs. Grabbing my t-shirt and jeans off the bathroom floor, I threw them back on. My poor feet ached too much for shoes, though. Marching out my door and then up the stairs, I came out onto the landing where the offending Penthouse Suite entrance stood. Gilded opulence practically oozed from the golden doorway. Knowing my luck, this was some rich frat boy who needed a lesson in civility.

I rang the doorbell and then pounded on the door for good measure. The volume of the music lowered just before the door opened. The man standing on the other side looked like sex made incarnate. As his eyes roamed over my body, I felt a crawling sensation run over my skin. *Something is off about this guy. Maybe this wasn't such a good idea.*

"Well, aren't you a tasty morsel. All rainbows and sunshine I see. Have you come to pay fealty to me or were you hoping to join in on my little party?"

I cocked my head sideways at the weird question. "Uhm. No. I came here to tell you to turn down your fucking music. Some of us paid a lot of money to come here and relax, but instead of being able to do that, we are standing barefoot on a cold ass marble floor arguing with some dickhead clearly violating all the noise ordinances for the whole of New York in the middle of the night."

I watched as this guy's lips curled up into a smirk. He was hot, and he knew it. But I still couldn't shake the crawling skin feeling. Something was very off here. *Who was this guy and what did he mean by paying him fealty?*

"You must either be incredibly stupid or extremely powerful to come here and yell at me. But I'll tell you what. If you come in and have a drink with me, I'll promise to keep the music down."

I scoffed as I crossed my arms over my chest. "How about no drink, you keep your music down, and we never see each other again?"

The unnamed sex god licked his lips. "I must say, you are a feisty one. While I do enjoy a challenge, I can assure you I always get what I want out of a deal."

The hairs on the back of my neck stood up, causing me to take an instinctive step back. "I haven't made any deals with the likes of you. Just keep your music down or I'll have to resort to drastic measures."

I moved to put more distance between me and this weirdo, but before I could get far enough away, his hand shot out and grabbed my arm, pulling me so hard I tumbled into his chest. Fear seized throughout my body as I felt a full-on panic attack starting. I tried wiggling free and even calling for my magic, but nothing was working. The more I fought, the bigger the mysterious man grinned.

"I am going to enjoy breaking the fight out of you. I don't know who sent you as a tribute, but I will reward them handsomely."

The guy tried to get me through the door while I tried to dig in my heels. I gained a little traction, getting my left foot braced against the doorjamb. I tried to take in several controlled breaths so I could negate the crushing panic clouding my mind. When I couldn't calm down, I called upon my magic once more, but nothing happened. I started losing my footing and was almost pulled into the guy's room until I felt arms wrap around my waist. In a moment, a cool autumn breeze wrapped itself around me, returning my breathing to normal. Relaxing, I fell back onto a familiar chest.

"Jasper Midnight. What in the ever-loving Fairy are you doing? Do you have any idea who this woman is?"

Jasper shrugged before wiggling his eyebrows and looking straight into my eyes. "She's the girl who was going to look good under me here in about twenty minutes. You know, after we had a nightcap and all."

A scowl formed over my face. I clenched my jaw so tight I could feel the muscles twitching. "In your dreams, you whacked out pervert. I only wanted you to turn your damned music off so I could take a nice hot bath. Now I'll have to take two baths just to get the filth of you off me."

"You see. She's a wildfire just begging to be tamed. Besides, I'm sure she's someone's tribute to me. I was only taking what they offered. What's it matter to you, Jax? Or should I call you, Your

Highness?" The creep smirked before dropping into an exaggerated bow.

"It matters because this wildfire you almost dragged into your penthouse against her will is not a tribute left for you. She is Princess Tempest Danvers of House Autumn. You know, the one who took down King Finvarra and Oberon? The tainted blood Fae who can talk to the dead and get them to tell her their darkest secrets. Hell, make her mad enough and she can channel the dead into the realm of the living. I was there as she brought her dead human sister's spirit to life in Fairy, without so much as trying. You wouldn't want Tempest to go looking for the ghosts in your closet, would you, Jasper? I mean, I'm sure your mother's angry spirit follows you around even now. What would you do if Tempest brought her back into this realm to torture you? I bet you'd rather just turn down your music, right?"

Jasper threw up both of his hands. "Woah, Jax. Easy there buddy. I didn't know she was your girl. And yeah, who hasn't heard of Princess Tempest? Even us exiles learned about what she did to break the curse on Fairy. I'm sorry I disrespected you, Princess. I guess your name fits you to the T. I'll keep the music down from now on, I promise. Just, please don't bring my mother back. I've only had a century of peace. I need about twenty more to recover from my childhood."

Jax growled. "I don't want to hear about you causing any more trouble, Jasper. If I do, I'm going to send Tempest to talk to you."

"Sure, I won't be a problem anymore. Hey, can you tell Aunt Morganna hello for me, but leave out the part where I tried to coerce the Princess, OK? I'd like to come back to Fairy at some point."

"I'm sure Mother would be happy to hear from you herself. Why don't you try picking up the communication orb every once in a while? It might help you get back into her good graces."

Jasper ran his hands through his hair, stopping to fidget with a curl. "Yeah, I'll call her tomorrow. Does she still have recess at the usual time?"

"Yup."

I felt Jax's arms pull me tighter against him before he scooped me up carrying me bridal style, turning us back towards the stairwell. Normally I would yell at him, but the conversation I witnessed preoccupied my brain too much. Plus, my feet really hurt now.

"Tempy, are you OK?"

Letting out a slow breath, I nodded. "Yeah, thanks to you."

"Good. Let's get you back to your suite. What's your room number?"

"The next floor down in suite 500."

"I'm glad I got here when I did. Jasper is a real jerk sometimes. Don't let him fool you. He knew exactly who you were and what he was doing."

"What exactly was he going to do with me?"

Jax smirked. "Seduce you to get a rise out of me."

My mouth fell open as I stared at Jax. "What now?"

"Every Fae these days knows the sad tale about the star-crossed lovers, Prince Jax and Princess Tempest. It's rather annoying. I have ladies showing up at my door all hours of the day and night trying to comfort the sad prince."

My mouth fell open as I tried to understand what Jax told me. "There's a story about us? When did this happen?"

"Right after your sister imported a shipment of your new book three months ago. And let me tell you, Maria did nothing to mitigate any rumors or conclusions drawn from the book. Next thing I know, I'm a helpless and heartbroken man of lore. I came back to the human world for a bit of a break."

"Right. All of that makes perfect sense, I think. I just don't understand why my magic wouldn't work. I tried to bring my power forth multiple times, but I felt like my magic was gone."

"My cousin Jasper has an ability to create wards to nullify magic. He's a dark Fae of House Winter. Ward Workers are nasty little boogers and often have whatever place they are staying at warded against magic. I'd say the door frame you put your foot on had some kind of nullification ward. He also has wards tattooed on his skin in Fae Ink."

"If he's related to you, I presume he is royalty. Why is he here wreaking havoc in the human realm?"

"Jasper is in exile for a little stunt he pulled back in Fairy about fifty years ago involving a bathhouse and a magic looking glass. He upset my mother a great deal and wound up here for an undetermined amount of time. Maybe one day I can tell you all about the tale."

"Great. Seems like I'm destined to run into trouble every time I step foot out of Kentucky. I've been here less than thirty-six hours and already had a fan boy trying to seduce me to get one over on the sad prince." I laughed. "To think this was supposed to be my grand adventure, to stand on my own two feet for once in my life. Do something I wanted. But look how that turned out! My feet hurt like hell and I'm currently not standing on them. I should just give up and go back home!"

"Why did you come back to New York, anyway? Last time I saw you, you seemed adamant about staying in your quaint southern home."

"I was born here in New York. Remember? When I came back to catch Maria's killer, I realized I missed this place. I kind of felt like I was finally home, but now I think the allure of this city may have dulled. Perhaps this vacation proves I don't need to buy a residence here because I don't belong anymore. I think Gamma Tempest was mistaken when she said New York was a comforting place for Fae to be. Or maybe it's just my tainted blood. I don't know. I guess there's nothing here for me anymore. Maybe I can try Arizona. I hear it's nice and dry there."

Jax's shoulders slumped the slightest bit as he nodded. When we reached suite 500, he sat me down on my feet. "Well, if you're sure you're not hurt, I'm going to head out. I'm working a double shift tonight and I have about ten more noise complaints to squash."

"Why are you here in New York instead of, you know, ruling? And why are you responding to noise complaints?" The questions were out of my mouth before I could stop the words.

"You mean besides hiding from groupies? Honestly, I wasn't ready to leave my human life behind. Mother thought a slower transition would be wise; so, she bent the rules for me. In a few weeks, I will officially retire as a full-time police officer and instead start a job as a consultant for the force. The consultant appointment will last for another year and then I'll see about going back to Fairy. These noise complaints are simply something to occupy my time since none of the other officers like to deal with these assignments."

I turned and unlocked the door before spinning back around, intending to say goodbye. Still feeling off from my encounter with Jasper, I turned too fast, my hand accidentally bumping into Jax's. A pure zap of energy shot through me, causing my body to tingle. The air filled with the scent of autumn winds; the scent calming my tattered nerves. Both the sensations and my reaction to him confused me. I held my breath, trying to demand the feelings to go away. "Thank you, Jax. It was nice to see you again. I hope everything works out with your transition. I'll try to talk to Maria about the mess she's made with the sad prince's tale."

Jax nodded, examining my face. His amber eyes glowed as he held my gaze. The tension in the space grew, but neither of us moved.

Finally, Jax smiled, but the smile didn't reach his eyes. "Likewise, Tempy. Try to stay away from trouble, you hear?"

I blushed while chewing on my lip, nodding all the while trying to ignore my heart attempting to beat out of my chest. I stood staring like an idiot as Jax turned to walk out of my life once again. My heart ached because, deep down, I knew this would be the last time I'd ever see him. I held my breath as I scolded myself for believing this ending was for the best, but then something primal from deep within bubbled up. *Was it for the best? Or was I lying to myself?* Before I could rethink my actions, I grabbed Jax's hand and pulled him through my room door, slamming the barrier behind us.

Jax raised his brow, questioning me. "Is something wrong?"

Fisting his shirt in both of my hands, I yanked him closer to me before crushing my lips to his. I let go of all the what ifs and allowed myself to simply feel. Kissing Jax was like kissing the autumn wind and rain. When his arms snaked around me returning the intensity of my kiss, I felt as if I had come home. I refused to break away until the very last of my breath left, forcing me to come up for air.

Jax sucked in his breath while touching his forehead to mine. "Wow, I've never been thanked for responding to a noise complaint like this before. What's gotten into you, Miss Danvers?"

"You, Mr. Dupree. You've worked your way under my skin quite thoroughly. In fact, I believe you have bewitched me, and I don't wish to be parted from you again. Besides, I can't stand by and let you keep being pegged as the helpless prince who lost his princess, can I?"

"Does this mean you are finally admitting to having real, curse free feelings for me?"

"You are all I think about these days, and the only logical solution I have found is the most illogical thing of all; I love you, Jax."

Jax towered above me, stroking my hair. "What exactly does our love look like to you? Does it only live in a quaint home in

223

Kentucky? A high rise here in New York? Or does our love live in Fairy?"

I shook my head. "I think our love will look like whatever we figure out together. I don't care where our love takes us. It's not as if there's only one place I can talk to ghosts or write books from. My magic lets me talk to Fae and human ghosts alike. Let's just call it a perk of being a tainted blood. It's time I started living for myself and getting the things I want. And right now, it's you I want, Jax."

Jax grasped my face in both of his hands as his thumbs stroked my cheeks. "Tempest Danvers, will you be my princess?"

My heart jumped and for the first time in a long time, joy coursed through my body. "Yes, Jax Dupree, but only if you will be my prince!"

Jax scooped me up into his arms before peppering my face with butterfly kisses. Leaning closer to my ear, his hot breath tickled my jaw as he spoke. "For all eternity."

THE END

Did you love *Murder in Loft 36: A Tempest Danvers Supernatural Tale*? Then you should read *To Kill A Siren*[1] by Shannon McRoberts!

Monsters Live Among Us Lexi River has one job---keep Gareth Blaze, a high -stakes gambler, out of trouble. It's an easy enough task for Lexi most of the time. That is until a mysterious woman named Genevieve bewitches Gareth into placing a bet he can't win.

Now penniless, Gareth and Lexi are forced to move back to their home state of Kentucky. Once there, they learn Gareth is being stalked by a supernatural creature called a Siren, and it won't stop until Gareth is dead.Can Lexi learn how to stop the Siren before it gets to Gareth?To Kill A Siren is the first book in a new urban

---

1. https://books2read.com/u/mVQwBA

2. https://books2read.com/u/mVQwBA

fantasy series that fans of Laurell K. Hamilton and Buffy alike are sure to enjoy.

Read more at www.shannonmcroberts.com.

Also by Shannon McRoberts

Monster Hunter Tales
To Stop A Fae
To Free A Djinn
To Kill A Siren

Poetry
Requiem For Dead Flowers
A Symphony Of Melancholy

Rebellious Romance
Contessa of Rebellion

The Daughter of Ares Chronicles
The Beginning: The Daughter of Ares Chronicles
The Narkurru
The Nikeda Trilogy
The Secret of Genetic Corp X
The Secret of Psi Corp X: Miranda's Tale

The Druidae Files
The Price of Magic

Standalone
Flavors of Fantasy
Murder in Loft 36: A Tempest Danvers Supernatural Tale

Watch for more at www.shannonmcroberts.com.

About the Author

Shannon McRoberts is a Creative Deconstructionist, weaving myths and lore into her works while living in the Bluegrass State of Kentucky. She is a USA Today Best-Selling author, artist, and poet focusing on works showcasing women, weapons, and magic. You can find out more, including contact and social media channels, by visiting https://sleek.bio/shannonmcroberts

Read more at www.shannonmcroberts.com.

About the Publisher

RGP is the imprint created by Shannon McRoberts, Head Creative Deconstructionist, to house all her creative endeavors.